Sherlock Holmes
and the
Abbey School Mystery

Sherlock Holmes
and the
Abbey School Mystery

John Hall

**BREESE
BOOKS
LONDON**

First published in 2001 by
Breese Books Ltd
164 Kensington Park Road, London W11 2ER, England

© Martin Breese, London, 2001

ISBN: 0 947533 249

Typeset in 11½/14pt Caslon by
Ann Buchan (Typesetters), Middlesex
Printed in the United States of America

This book is dedicated to
Abbot Roger de Jourdain,
not forgetting Anne

PROLEGOMENA

All things bright and beautiful,
All creatures great and small,
All things wise and wonderful,
The Lord God made them all.

As the singing died away and the atmosphere became slightly more relaxed, the headmaster, Dr Thomas Longton, stepped forward to the great oak lectern with the eagle's head jutting out from it.

'Never known Long Tom look so furious,' muttered Watson Minor to Edmonds, who stood beside him in the ranks of the Third.

'Silence!' Dr Longton's voice fairly roared out, filling the great assembly hall. His big hands gripped the eagle's wings, as if for support, and his gaze travelled round the assembly, seeming to rest for a moment on each boy. Some there were who avoided that basilisk stare, perhaps for some guilty reason known only to the boy concerned, perhaps because they merely feared what was to come, felt that dread of the unknown which all of us have experienced at some time or another. But most of them met Dr Longton's gaze fair and square, and merely wondered what on earth the head was going to tell them.

'Boys, the usual announcements will be suspended this morning.'

At the back of the hall, the prefects of the Upper Sixth exchanged discreet glances, a raised eyebrow here, a pursing of the lips there, an occasional shrug of the shoulders so slight as to be almost undetectable. Two rows in front of these demi-gods, Watson Major of the Lower Sixth muttered to Meade, at his side, 'I knew it! Trouble ahead, mark my words.' Those who had been at the Abbey School any length of time knew the formula by now. Any suspension of the usual announcements at morning assembly meant a serious breach of the school rules had been committed, and that usually meant expulsion. And that was the end. There were other schools, it is true, with less rigorous codes, but there was none quite like the Abbey School.

Dr Longton took a deep breath before going on. 'It pains me to have to tell you that a very serious crime has been committed. A sum of money has been stolen from one of the masters.' Dr Longton paused. 'I should be much obliged if the thief would step forward now, before this assembly, so that all may know him.'

He stared at the great stained glass window, waiting. No-one spoke, there was no sound save an isolated clearing of a young throat here and there, and the occasional shuffle of feet which would not keep still.

'I may say that the culprit, the thief, as I have more accurately called him, is known to me,' Dr Longton added after what seemed an eternity.

Further aeons passed, and it was a relief to most of those there when Dr Longton eventually said, 'In that event, I should like to see Whitechurch in my study immediately after this assembly.'

'Crikey!' Watson Minor simply could not help himself,

though he was sure that the word was inaudible to anyone more than a yard away.

'And that boy! Watson Minor. In my study, at morning break.' Dr Longton's voice crashed out and echoed from the very walls.

Watson Minor grimaced, hearing the cane swishing down towards his trouser seat already.

'Bad luck, old man,' mumbled Edmonds.

'And that boy, too. Edmonds. Morning break.' And Dr Longton turned and swept from the dais, the rest of the masters following, as old Mr Donaldson, the music master, struck up a rousing rendition of 'For those in peril on the sea' on the piano.

'It's us that's in peril,' said Watson Minor more or less ungrammatically, but with great emotion none the less.

'Worse things happen at sea, they say.' Edmonds tried to look unconcerned.

As they filed out from assembly in strict order of seniority, Watson Major, lurking by the door, stepped forward and took hold of his brother's ear in none too gentle a fashion. 'You young ass! What the devil d'you mean by speaking out like that?'

'Ow! Nothing, Bertie – I mean, Watson Major. But, Whitechurch! I can't believe it, can you?'

'It is devilish odd,' admitted Watson Major, releasing his brother before too much harm was done. 'And you had the devil's own nerve to speak up,' he added, a note of admiration apparent in his voice. 'Even if you will pay for it with a sore backside.' He frowned. 'But it is devilish odd, youngster, just as you say. I tell you something else, that's not the only odd thing going on round here at the moment.'

'What do you mean?' asked Edmonds curiously.

'Never you mind,' said Watson Major darkly, as if he could tell strange stories if he would.

Edmonds exchanged a glance with Watson Minor. 'You know,' he said awkwardly, 'Mr Greville was saying something of that sort the other day.'

'Oh?' Mr Greville was the Third's form master, a youngish man who had always struck Watson Major as more approachable than many of the other masters. 'What did old Greville say, then?'

'Oh, I don't know,' said Edmonds, a vague feeling that he was being something of a sneak preventing any further disclosure.

'You must know, or you wouldn't have said it,' Watson Major pointed out.

'Well, but you won't tell anyone I said anything?'

'You little wretch!'

'Sorry, Watson Major. Well, someone had cheeked him, or something. I think it was old "Pie Can" – that's Potter, you know – and Mr Greville muttered something like, "The Abbey School's going to the –" that word you used just now.'

'The one Papa says you mustn't use,' added Watson Minor helpfully.

'Oh, that's nothing special,' said Watson Major. 'Anyone might say that sort of thing if you young devils had cheeked him.'

'No,' said Edmonds, 'but then Mr Greville went on, "It's getting out of hand, and something should be done", or something of that sort.'

'And he said that to you?' asked Watson Major, impressed.

'Well, he didn't actually say it *to* me, of course, he sort of mumbled it to himself as he passed me, and I said, "Beg pardon, sir?" and he sort of jumped, and said, "Sorry, my boy", like he does, "talking to myself. Touch of indigestion, I fear", and he gave me two bob and sent me to the village shop to buy a box of little liver pills, the one and threepence size, and told me to keep the change.'

'I see.' Watson Major stared into space for a long moment. 'Old Greville, eh? I –' he stopped as the bell rang. 'Anyway, it's class, so don't dawdle. You two are in enough trouble as it is.'

'But do you think Whitechurch did it?' Edmonds persisted.

'I'm damned if I can see why he should, for his father's about the richest man in England. But it isn't up to me. If I were you, lads, I'd look for a new chum.' As they started down the corridor, Watson Major frowned, and called after them, 'Hey! Don't talk about this with anyone else.'

*

'Please take a seat, Your Grace.' Mr Sherlock Holmes ushered the Duke of Greyminster to a chair. 'May I offer you a cigar? A glass of brandy?'

'A very small brandy would be welcome, Mr Holmes, for I confess my nerves are considerably shaken.' The duke took his drink, nodded his thanks, and stared at Holmes for a long while before continuing. 'Mr Holmes, the matter upon which I have come to consult you is a very delicate one, and I must begin by asking you to maintain the utmost discretion.'

'You have my assurance, sir.'

'The matter concerns my only child, Lord Whitechurch. Have you ever heard of the Abbey School, Mr Holmes?'

Holmes frowned, shook his head, then nodded and said, 'Ah, I believe I have heard something of it. A small but very exclusive private establishment, is it not?'

'That is it exactly, Mr Holmes. I am scarcely surprised that the name is not immediately familiar even to you, for the exclusive nature of the place is its keynote. The boys who attend the school are from the finest families in the land, and indeed from overseas. I myself was a pupil there, as a matter of fact. But make no mistake, Mr Holmes, mere cash alone is insufficient to gain entry to the Abbey School. There is no place there for the *nouveau riche*, the outsider who thinks money answers all things. A family connection, or some personal recommendation, is essential before ever a boy can be considered as a pupil. It is not uncommon for old boys to put forward the name of their son at birth, to be certain of securing his acceptance.'

'I see.' Holmes took out an ancient pipe, thought better of it, replaced the pipe in his pocket and took out a cigar case, which he offered to the duke. 'And your son, Lord Whitechurch, is a pupil there?'

The duke frowned, and took time to light his cigar before he answered. 'He *was* a pupil at the Abbey School, Mr Holmes. He was expelled a couple of days ago.'

'Indeed?'

'That is why I have come to consult you, Mr Holmes.'

Holmes smiled. 'I appreciate the gravity of the situation, Your Grace, but I am no dominie. Would you not be better consulting the College of Preceptors, or whatever the appropriate body may be?'

'It was not because of any fault in his studies that he was expelled, Mr Holmes. He was accused of theft.'

'Ah.' Holmes leaned forward in his chair. He produced

the pipe again, and waved it. 'You have no objection? Thank you. That, of course, is a different matter. What was he accused of stealing, exactly?'

'Twenty-five pounds in Bank of England notes.'

'Dear me! From a fellow pupil?'

'No, Mr Holmes, from the headmaster himself. From the headmaster's study, in fact.'

'Dear me!' said Holmes a second time. He leaned back in his chair. 'That is surely unusual, in my admittedly limited experience.'

The duke gave a short and mirthless bark of laughter. 'It is unbelievable, Mr Holmes. Particularly when you consider that in order to reach the headmaster's study a thief would be obliged to pass through an outer room occupied by the school secretary, a young man named Carstairs.'

'The theft occurred through the day, when the secretary would normally be at his duties?'

The duke nodded. 'So it is said.'

'H'mm. Presumably your son is supposed to have entered the study during a break of some sort, when the headmaster and secretary might both be expected to be taking tea in the Common Room, or something of the sort?'

The duke shrugged. 'I cannot very well speculate as to that, sir. Frankly, I had not given any thought to what one might term the mechanism of the theft, since I am quite convinced that my son did not commit it.'

'I quite understand. Of course, if a theft were committed, and your son is not the guilty party, then the thief must be someone else, and there is a pretty obvious suspect.'

'The secretary, Carstairs, you mean?'

Holmes nodded. 'He surely had a better opportunity than anyone else.'

'It maybe an obvious conclusion, Mr Holmes, but I assure you that it is incorrect. Why, I know the young man personally. His father is the vicar of my own parish, and I myself was instrumental in securing the secretary's post for the young man. I would trust him with my life, as the saying is.'

'Perhaps so, Your Grace. But it would not be the first time that a young man, away from the family home and the guiding hand of a father, has strayed from the path of righteousness, would it? Even if he is a vicar's son.'

Again the duke shook his head, more angrily this time. 'It is not the first time he has been away from home, though. He was three years at university, and there was never the least hint of impropriety. Why, he read Theology!'

Holmes frowned.

'To suggest that Carstairs had found a taste for gambling, or got some village girl into trouble! Why, it is quite preposterous,' the duke went on. 'And besides, if he had done so, if he had suddenly needed money, he could have come to me, even if the matter were of such delicacy that he could not approach his father. I flatter myself that I am a man of the world, sir.'

'There are matters which are hardly fit for discussion even with a man of the world,' said Holmes, though without much conviction in his tone.

'Nonsense! He could have talked to me about anything, and he knows it. And then, if he had taken this trifling sum, why should he attempt to put the blame on my son?'

'No other thefts have taken place at the Abbey School?'

'None, sir. Or at least none that I know of. The school's reputation is, and always has been, of the highest. '

'Well, let us for the sake of argument suppose for a moment that some sudden crisis had occurred in this young man's life. In a moment of weakness he steals the money.'

'Bank of England notes, the numbers of which can be traced with ease?' the duke broke in sceptically.

Holmes waved a hand. 'The same objection applies to the notion that your son took the money. How old is the boy?'

'Fourteen.'

'So he is old enough to know that currency notes are easily identified. Let us continue. This Carstairs takes the money, and the headmaster discovers the theft. Carstairs comes to his sense, realizes that the notes could be traced to him, he wants to return them, but he cannot return them because it is too late.'

'Why, then could he not simply burn them?' asked the duke. 'There are fires burning at this season. Easy enough to lean forward to the flames – presto! As the magicians have it.'

'He may simply not have thought of that. A man who feels he is under attack, whose brain is under unusual exertion because of disturbing circumstances, does not always think clearly.'

'But then why put the blame on my son, who is almost a brother to him? Why not choose to implicate some stranger?'

'H'mm. I wonder if there is anything there? Was this Carstairs perhaps too much like a son to you, Your Grace? May he not have felt some jealousy towards your real son? Envy at your own wealth and position?'

The duke shook his head impatiently. 'No, Mr Holmes, you are quite wrong there. Carstairs is a perfectly ordinary young man, save that he has advantages which most young men do not possess.'

'But you said, I think, that you had secured him the post

of secretary?'

'Ah, but that was merely a word to the school authorities. And my recommendation would have meant nothing without the young man's own academic entitlements and successes. No, Mr Holmes, Carstairs regards me as a patron, and, I trust, as a friend of sorts, but he definitely does not regard me as a father, and neither does he feel any jealousy towards my son. Why, Carstairs wrote me a most moving and dignified letter after the unfortunate expulsion, saying that he could never believe my son guilty, and that the whole business must be some tragic error.'

'I see.' Holmes stared at the ceiling for a while. 'Let us proceed to another point. How came the theft to be laid at your son's door?'

'Ah, that is another curious point. It is alleged that he was seen leaving the study, and a search of my son's possessions revealed the cash.'

'Alleged? And by whom was he seen?'

'That I cannot tell you. I very naturally asked, but Dr Longton, the headmaster, said that he could not betray a confidence.'

'He did not indicate whether it was a master, or a pupil?' The duke shook his head.

Holmes put another match to his pipe, leaned back and stared at the ceiling. For a long time he sat there, with only an occasional puff of blue smoke from his pipe being the only animated thing about him. Eventually he pulled himself together with a perceptible start, and looked at the duke, though still without speaking. 'Well, Your Grace,' he said at last, ' I fear that I am unable to accept your case.'

'Mr Holmes, you disappoint me greatly.'

'My advice to you is to find another school for Lord

Whitechurch, and forget this matter, if you can.'

The duke shook his head. 'I fear I can scarcely be expected to do that, Mr Holmes.'

'It would be best if you did.'

There was something in Holmes's tone that made the duke ask, 'Do you suspect that my son is guilty after all, then, Mr Holmes?'

'I did not say that.'

'But yet you suspect it?'

'Well, since you put the question plainly,' said Holmes, 'this Carstairs may not be the only young man to need cash in a hurry.'

'Impossible,' said the duke angrily. 'My son has plenty of money. The school limits the amount of pocket money – a weekly stipend is allowed to each boy – the idea being that no one boy should indulge in an ostentatious display of wealth before the others. But my son knows that a telegram to me would secure any amount in an emergency.'

'Even an emergency that he could not discuss with Your Grace?'

'I can see what you are thinking, Mr Holmes, but I assure you that you are wrong in that. Why, if some emergency, as we are calling it, some crisis, had occurred, it would not go away merely because my son has been expelled. And he has not asked for any money from me since he came home.'

'H'mm. But I still cannot think that an investigation would produce any result satisfactory to Your Grace. Could you face the truth if your son were, indeed, guilty?'

The duke started to speak, but Holmes held up a hand, and went on, 'If your son is innocent, and I am happy to accept your assertion that he is, then I think that the real thief has muddied the waters so effectively that the truth will never be known. And what if it were? What if I found the real thief? True, your son might be reinstated, but he would face the charge of being a sneak, of making trouble with the authorities instead of accepting his punishment, justified or not, and there is no more serious charge that one schoolboy can level against another. His position would be unenviable, if not downright untenable. Guilty or not, your son can never hope to return to the Abbey School as if naught had happened. I can only repeat my advice. Find another school, and put this sad business out of your mind.'

The duke stood up. 'Frankly, I had hoped for more, Mr Holmes. But I see that you are very likely correct in your reading.' He held out his hand. 'Thank you, sir. There merely remains the matter of your fee?'

Holmes waved a hand. 'I have done no more than any friend would do, Your Grace, and that is give you my honest opinion. I trust your son's future will not be too badly affected by this sorry affair.'

The duke shook Holmes's hand a second time, then collected his coat and hat and went out. Holmes resumed his seat. He refilled his pipe, and smoked quietly for a time. Then he sighed, and said 'Damnable!' to himself. He stood up and took a large notebook from a shelf, found a pen amongst the debris on the table, and riffled through the book until he found a blank page. He thought for a moment, then dipped the pen in the inkwell, and wrote at the top of the page, 'The Abbey School.'

*

The room had been intended for three pupils, but the abrupt departure of Lord Whitechurch meant that it was temporarily occupied only by Edmonds and Watson Minor. This should have created a cosier atmosphere, but Edmonds for one felt that it had the opposite effect. Matters were not helped by the fact that although it was now December there was no fire in the room. The moon, shining through the leaded window, lit the place up but the light was cold, cheerless, even sinister. Edmonds shivered, and nestled further down into his blankets.

'Come on, you idle dog.' Watson Major, fully dressed, pulled Edmonds's blankets off him.

'Oh, you don't really mean to go outside tonight?'

'I told you,' said Watson Minor, 'I know old Greville is planning something. He's been muttering to himself all day, as he does, and I'm sure I heard him say, "Tonight's the night", as he passed me this morning.'

'It was most probably a quotation from Shakespeare, or somebody,' Edmonds pointed out, trying to retrieve his blankets.

'Whereabouts in Shakespeare does it say, "Tonight's the night", then?'

'Oh, I don't know. *Macbeth*, the scene with the witches.'

'Does it? Anyway, I'm going out to see what happens.'

'We're in enough trouble as it is, you know. I don't relish the notion of another whacking quite so soon.'

'Oh, well. I don't care. You stay there if you're scared.'

'Who says I'm scared? Who's scared? I'm not scared. I'll go, of course. Only I don't think anything will happen,' said Edmonds, cautiously lowering his feet on to the cold floor and reaching for his clothes.

The two boys made their way quietly to the door of the room. Silence was essential, for, although the room had no other occupant, a prefect slept on each landing and by tradition the door of the prefect's room was left open at night, the better to alert the prefect to any emergency such as a fire, or – far more likely – some intended nocturnal adventure such at the present one.

Edmonds carefully opened the door, and the two went out into the corridor, closing the door behind them so that their absence was not quite so noticeable.

For almost an hour the room remained empty and silent. The moonlight that had shone on the door now shone on one of the three beds. Then the door opened slowly, and two small figures crept inside.

'Well,' said Edmonds, crawling back into bed with no attempt to change back into his pyjamas, 'I'm *so* glad that I didn't let you talk me into staying here. I really wouldn't have missed that for the world.'

'It wasn't my fault,' Watson Minor pointed out. 'I honestly thought that something interesting would happen tonight. And Herbert, my brother, you know, he's convinced that something's wrong, and I thought – well. Sorry,' he added lamely.

'Think nothing of it, old man. But please let me try to get an hour's sleep, would you? There's a good chap.'

Silence returned to the room for a further hour. Then Edmonds sat bolt upright in his bed. 'What was that, Watson?'

'Well, it wasn't me.' Watson Minor, half awake, struggled to a sitting position. 'What's the matter Edmonds? What was what?'

'I thought I heard something. Sorry. Must have been all the excitement earlier, making me restless.'

'Well, but what did you think you heard?'

'I don't know. A sort of bump.'

'Oh, "things that go bump in the night", was it?'

'Now, that *is* from *Macbeth*.' There was the sound of a match being struck, and a flare of light cast deep shadows.

'What are you doing now?'

'Just checking my watch. I want to know how much longer we've got before we have to get up.'

'Go back to sleep, Edmonds.'

*

'I say, have you heard about Mr Greville?' asked Merton, stuttering with excitement.

'What about him, then?' asked Watson Minor, rubbing the sleep from his eyes.

'He's dead!'

'Dead? What rot! How can he be dead? Why –' and Watson Minor broke off as the form room door opened.

It was not Mr Greville who entered, though, but Dr Longton, looking very grave. 'Sit down, boys,' he told them, as they got to their feet. He looked round the room, and sighed aloud. 'Boys, I regret that I have some tragic news for you. Doubtless some of you will have heard a rumour, and in any case I shall be announcing it before the whole school at assembly, so you, being the Third, had best hear it from me now. There has been a tragic accident, a dreadful accident, late last night. Mr Greville –' he broke off, as if overcome by some powerful emotion, and only recovered himself with a palpable effort. 'I have to tell you that Mr Greville is dead. A tragic accident,' he repeated.

There was a murmur of conversation, which Dr Longton, contrary to his usual custom, did not at once stop. It seemed that he understood their fears and confusion, and perhaps even shared them. But after a moment he held up a hand for silence, and went on, 'Since the end of term is but a week or so off, I shall take over as form master for the Third, on a strictly temporary basis. I hope to have a replacement early next year.' He took up the register and a pen, and began to call the roll.

At the back of the class, Edmonds and Watson Minor exchanged a glance that was full of meaning.

ONE

In the summer of 1902 I left the rooms at 221B Baker Street which I had shared for so long with Mr Sherlock Holmes, and moved into apartments in Queen Anne Street. It was not that Holmes and I were no longer friends, we had not quarrelled or anything silly of that sort. No, the fact was that after a decade of being a widower, I had at last met a lady who might be compared, in my opinion at any rate, to my dear departed Mary. After a lengthy acquaintance, I ventured to make my feelings known, and was delighted to find that they were reciprocated. I asked the lady if she would do me the honour of becoming my wife, and she agreed. As I say, I moved house in summer, a month or so before the wedding, and remarried in early autumn.

I had determined that I would not do as I had done in my first marriage, when I had spent half my time – or so it seemed – with Holmes. Not, as I say, that I have anything against Holmes. He is the best friend I have in all the world, and I trust that he always will be. But his cases, always so intriguing and absorbing, had taken me away from Mary more times than I cared, or dared, to remember, and I did not wish to repeat the process with my second wife.

Moreover, if I am to be entirely honest, my second wife

had intimated, albeit with great delicacy, that she would not take too kindly to being thus neglected for Holmes.

I therefore decided that the break with Holmes was to be complete and final. My home life would be my own, and I should not even mention my wife's name in print. Those who know us socially know her name; and as far as those who do not know us socially are concerned, well, quite frankly it is none of their business.

I still saw Holmes occasionally, of course, but these occasions were few and far between. He attended the wedding, with a look of regret upon his face which might have cast a gloom over the event, but did not. And then I saw him perhaps two or three times before the end of the year. I enjoyed these infrequent meetings, and always asked for news of his current cases. I even ventured to give my opinion on some of them, although Holmes seemed not to attach too much weight to my words.

I intended that my days were to be spent in work, but this time I had not returned to medicine, for life had left me with no illusions about my abilities or experience. I knew that I had been out of practice, in every sense of the phrase, for a very long time, and that although I was, or so I flattered myself, a competent family practitioner, I had no special expertise. And I had to confess to myself that I was now too old to take over a run-down practice and work it up, as I had done years before at the time of my first marriage. True, I might have bought a practice in a more fashionable quarter and relied upon my reputation, a reputation which writing about Holmes had brought me, to attract wealthy patients, but that smacked of fraud. And there was another, a more powerful reason. The success which I had enjoyed with my accounts of Holmes's cases had convinced me that my real talents lay not in medicine but in writing, and I accordingly determined to devote my days to the production of books which would truly count as Literature, with a capital 'L'.

I very soon found that this was much easier said than done. After some weeks of that contemplation which the cynical might call idleness, I decided that historical fiction would be my choice. I then had to narrow down the vast field, electing finally to deal with English history in the medieval period; more specifically still, the period of Agincourt and the stirring deeds of chivalry and bravery performed by the courtly knights. My knowledge of this period being somewhat limited, I began by reading up as many books as I could find in the libraries. Rather like Mr Jabez Wilson on another occasion, I soon knew all that had been written on Archers, and Battles, and Castles, and I promised myself that I should make a start on my *magnum opus* early in the new year.

Christmas came, and we held a modest celebration, my wife and I, just the two of us. We saw in 1903, and I stocked my desk with paper and pencils, pens and ink, and tried to settle down to make a start. Now, I have never had the least trouble with writing about Holmes, I simply think back to what happened, and set it down on paper. But this was different. I knew that once I had the introductory paragraph finished, the rest would be easy, but for some absurd reason that first paragraph simply would not let itself be written.

For two days I sat at my desk, writing a word or two, perhaps as much as a whole sentence, then rolling the foolscap sheet into a ball and hurling it into the waste paper basket. Early on the morning of the third day, I settled down, determined that today I should make a proper start. For an hour I stared at the blank sheet. Two hours. I lit my pipe, and stared out of the window, turning with a start when the maid tapped at the door and looked in.

'Beg pardon, Doctor, but there's Mr Holmes here to see you.'

Never was I more glad to see a man in all my life. 'My dear Holmes,' I cried, 'come in and sit down! A cigar? Brandy?'

'Thank you, I will have a cigar,' said Holmes, 'though I fear that your literary habits are a little too fast for me. Ten in the morning is just a trifle early for brandy.'

'Well, I was merely being hospitable,' I told him, with a sad glance at the decanter. 'Too early for me too, of course. Now, what is the case upon which you wish to have my opinion?'

'Remarkable, Watson!' he said with a laugh. 'How did you know I wanted your opinion on a case?'

'It is an elementary deduction,' I told him. 'Even your bohemian outlook cannot possibly see ten in the morning as being the correct hour for a social call. And besides, there is an indefinable look about you, Holmes. Like an old foxhound which sees the huntsman raise the horn, and knows the chase is about to begin.'

He laughed again. 'You are right, Watson.' He leaned forward, and grew serious. 'Now, my boy, have you ever heard of the Abbey School?'

'The name is not entirely unfamiliar. A private school, one of the more exclusive, is it not?'

'One of the most exclusive. Then you have not heard of the tragedy which took place at the school quite recently?'

I shook my head.

'It was kept out of the press,' said Holmes, 'although the local newspaper had a short report of the inquest. One of the masters, a young man named Greville, who had charge of the Third form, went out late at night, climbed to the top of a tower affair which overlooks the school quadrangle, and apparently threw himself off into space. His head was dreadfully injured, as you would expect, so that death must have occurred more or less instantaneously as he hit the ground.'

'Good Lord! Suicide?'

'The coroner's verdict was "accidental death", but I gather that the general consensus is that he was trying to spare the young man's family any further distress. Suicide is the general opinion, and I confess that I can see no satisfactory alternative.'

'And the cause? Had he any financial worries? A failed romance, perhaps?'

'You anticipate, Watson.' Holmes sat back in his chair. 'The Abbey School first came to my attention early in December last year, when I was consulted by the Duke of Greyminster, whose son had recently been expelled.'

'But what has that to do with the young man's death?' I asked, puzzled.

Holmes cast an impatient glance at me. 'That is one of the points which I find intriguing, Watson. But please bear with me. The duke's son, Lord Whitechurch, had been expelled after being accused of theft, and theft of Bank of England notes at that, in odd circumstances.'

'That is odd.'

Another impatient glance from Holmes silenced me. 'Well, there seemed nothing I could do, and so I advised the duke to find another school for the boy, and put the matter out of his mind.'

'But you did not put it out of yours, I gather.'

Holmes laughed. 'Indeed not. The odd, the unusual, always appeals to me. I made a note of the matter, then, against such time as I should hear of the Abbey School again.'

'Which you thought likely?'

'Where there is one odd occurrence, there may well be others. And I was right, you see, for this other curious business, the death of young Greville, occurred a mere week or so later.'

'You intrigue me,' I said, leaning forward.

'The second matter came to my attention when the young man's sister, Miss Greville, came to see me. She was naturally upset at her brother's death, but more particularly since the circumstances seemed to her to be so very curious. To begin with, there was no obvious reason why he should wish to kill himself. His father is manager of a branch of the Capital and Counties Bank, and the family, although not excessively wealthy, is in very comfortable circumstances. In fact, his father had given young Greville a present of three hundred pounds two years ago, when the young man took up his post at the school. Some two hundred and fifty pounds remain in that account, and the bills for clothing, golf clubs, and the like, all bought at the start of his time at the school, explain all but ten or twelve pounds.'

'Fitting himself out for his new career, then?'

'As you say. Once he was earning money from teaching, he appears to have lived on that, and even managed to save a few pounds each quarter, which he deposited into another account, his intention apparently being to save enough for a lengthy visit to the Continent in the summer holidays.

He has never made a withdrawal from this second account. Money troubles, therefore, may be safely ruled out.'

'Romance, then?'

'He had formed some attachment with the daughter of a friend of his father's, and they were to announce their engagement later in the year.'

'H'mm. No obvious reason why he should wish to kill himself, then.'

'Another thing which puzzled Miss Greville was that the body had a strong smell of whisky.'

'Nerving himself up for the task? Nothing odd in that, if he did kill himself.'

'An obvious reading, Watson. But apparently whisky did not agree with him, and he never drank it. Indeed, Miss Greville assures me that he seldom touched spirits of any kind, and then only brandy and soda, very weak.'

'Ah, but that doesn't follow,' I said. 'Even a man who never drinks at all may well feel the need of fortification if he is contemplating some serious enterprise. And you don't get much more serious than suicide, after all.'

'Oh, I agree. It is inconclusive, but it is odd, none the less.' Holmes leaned forward again and stared at me. 'There is one last oddity, Watson. I have said that the young man fell from a tower in the school yard. Miss Greville told me that, from being a boy, he was afraid of heights! What do you say to that?'

'Well,' I said doubtfully, 'if he were contemplating making away with himself, and he had settled on that method, that might explain the whisky?'

Holmes shook his head. 'It is all very puzzling,' he said.

'What about this? This young man is scared of heights, and feels ashamed of his fears, so he decides to face them by climbing this tower. He does so at night, so that nobody will see him if he succumbs to his terrors, but at the last minute he loses his nerve, and seeks courage from the bottle. Thus fortified, he does indeed climb the tower, but is overcome by vertigo at the top, or perhaps the whisky has deprived him of his sense of balance? That might be the answer.'

'H'mm. It is certainly a very thorough explanation, Watson, and I might have been inclined to think that the truth lies that way. But I had listened to Miss Greville, you see, and I was impressed by her testimony. I had to earn my fee, and so I went along to the Abbey School to ask a few questions of my own.'

'And?' I asked, for Holmes seemed to hesitate.

'And I am sure that they are hiding something. Not in concert, I do not claim that they are all in any sort of conspiracy, but there seemed an overall air of reticence, a reluctance on the part of boys and masters alike to answer any of my questions.'

'That's not so difficult to understand, though, Holmes. The boys would be embarrassed at something that involves one of their masters, while the masters would not want to dwell on anything that reflected badly on the school as a whole.'

'Oh, I agree that a certain amount of discomfort, discomposure, was to be expected, a certain desire not to say too much out of school, so to speak. But it went beyond that, or I am much mistaken, Watson. The headmaster, Dr Longton, was positively short with me, he told me that he hadn't asked my opinion, he questioned the legality of my asking questions –'

'About time someone did! You do rather usurp the function of the official police at times, Holmes.'

He laughed at this. 'You may be right. Dr Longton was, of course, well within his rights to refuse to speak to me. But none the less, I had the distinct impression that it went deeper.'

'You actually suspect the headmaster of the most exclusive school in England of being implicated in some skulduggery?'

'I do not say that. But I am far from satisfied, Watson.'

We smoked in silence for a time, then I said, 'But, Holmes, if it were not an accident, and it were not suicide, then that rather narrows the field down, does it not?'

Holmes nodded, but said nothing.

'Really, Holmes! Who on earth would want to kill a young schoolmaster? Was he popular with his fellow masters, and the boys?'

Holmes nodded. 'He was well liked by everyone, it seems.'

'There you are, then. No money worries, no enemies. Not the picture of a murder victim, Holmes.'

'Nor of a suicide?'

I frowned. 'No, I accept that, and I believe that the verdict was correct, that it was some tragic accident. I have already suggested that the young man was attempting to confront his fear of heights, and that it went tragically wrong. That is, I think, the only logical explanation.'

'And I think you are wrong, Watson, although I could not begin to tell you why I think so. All my instincts tell me that there is more to it than meets the eye. And that is why I have come to consult you.'

'I am flattered, Holmes. I am only sorry that I have not been able to help more.'

'Ah.' He had the grace to look embarrassed.

'Oh, I see! You want practical help, rather than just

advice, is that it? Well, I had planned to start my next novel this week, but I'm sure that I can spare a day, or even two, if that will serve.'

Holmes studied the toes of his boots with some care. 'The fact is, Watson, I was rather hoping for a little more than that. The difficulty is, you see, that I have already been to the school, I am known to them.'

'Oh, I see, you want me to go there alone? Well –'

'No, no.' He waved me to silence with an impatient gesture. 'You cannot be identified as a colleague of mine, or they will simply close ranks again.'

'But what reason, what justification, would I have for going there and asking questions, other than as an associate of yours?'

Holmes sighed. 'The headmaster has not yet replaced the dead man, Greville. The Third form still lacks a form master, and the school as a whole lacks an English teacher. I need a reliable man on the inside, and there is no better man than you. The headmaster, as I say, is pretty desperate to find someone, as it is halfway through the academic year and there are few masters looking for posts just now. A word from the Duke of Greyminster would secure the post for you. You will need another name, of course, that of John H Watson is too well known, but I shall leave that to you.'

'Good Lord! Are you joking, Holmes?'

'I was never more serious, Watson.'

'But – well, for one thing, I know nothing at all about teaching. I have no qualifications, no experience.'

Holmes waved a hand dismissively. 'How difficult can it be? As to qualifications, you have written many short stories for the popular press, several books about me which certainly deserve the title "imaginative fiction", and I don't know what else. If that is not sufficient qualification to teach English, then pray what is?' He waved his hand round my little study. 'What is more, if more were needed, I see by the very many slips of paper marking your place in these books that you have been doing some heavy research into the world of letters. Now, honestly, can you think of a man better qualified for the task?'

'It is true that I have been reading up on English history,' I admitted.

'And chiefly its fictional representations, I see.'

'Much easier to read than dry old text books, Holmes.'

'Then will you not give it a try? It may be of the first importance, Watson. I have said that the Abbey School is an exclusive establishment, but perhaps I have not made clear to you just how exclusive it really is.' He produced a memorandum book and opened it, passing it across to me. 'That is a list of just a dozen or so of the boys currently at the school, with the names and occupations of their fathers.'

I glanced through his list. There was a cabinet minister, two bishops, various captains of industry whose doings were reported almost daily in the popular press. And against one entry with a foreign name Holmes had laconically noted the father's occupation as, 'King'.

'These are impressive names, Holmes. Some of the richest, most famous men in the entire world evidently send their sons to the place.'

He nodded. 'You see now why we must find out if anything is not what it should be?'

'But, Holmes, even if I were ten, twenty, times better qualified than is the case, there is another, a more weighty, reason why I cannot do as you ask.'

'Oh? And what may that be, then?'

I could see there was no help for it. Holmes was not in any mood to be satisfied with half-truths. And so I gritted my teeth, metaphorically speaking, and told him some of the reasons why I could not help him, very much on the lines which I have set down at the beginning of this chapter, although I had to soften it a bit for his sake.

He heard me out in silence, then got to his feet. 'I quite understand,' he said. 'It is for the best, after all. You have your new life, your new family.' He sighed. 'I grow old, Watson. I tell you, I have been very seriously considering my own retirement.'

'Surely, not, Holmes?'

'I have. There is no relish in the work any more, my boy. Not since you – well, let us not dwell on that.'

'And this business of the Abbey School, Holmes?'

'Oh, I shall just have to let the matter drop. Very likely it is as you say, the whole matter was a tragic accident.' And he shook my hand, helped himself to another of my cigars, and saw himself out, leaving me floundering in my study pretty much open-mouthed.

Dear reader, I do not know what you would have thought under the circumstances. I only know that I felt the most heartless, miserable cur under the sun, a worthless wretch indifferent to his fellow man. A dozen times I started up from my chair and set off towards the telephone in the lobby, meaning to tell Holmes that I had changed my mind. And a dozen times I sat down again, resolved to keep the promise which I had made to myself when I remarried. It was unfortunate to have to let Holmes down, I told myself, and it would be a fine thing to work with Holmes one last time, but my mind was made up. Needless to say, I abandoned any hopes of starting my novel for the day, and sat smoking pipe after pipe in gloomy abstraction.

When the luncheon hour came round, I was in a dismal mood. But as soon as I saw my wife's expression, I forgot my own petty problems, for trouble was writ large on her lovely face. 'What is it?' I asked at once.

'Oh, it is Elizabeth. She saw your man.'

I knew at once what my wife meant. The lady she mentioned was a widow, an old friend of my wife's, and had consulted me in a professional capacity after feeling unwell for some time. I had not liked what I saw, and referred her to a colleague for a second opinion. 'Bad news, then?'

My wife produced a letter. 'It is as you thought. Consumption.'

'Ah.'

'But your friend is quite optimistic. He says that six weeks in Egypt will work wonders.'

'Oh, well, that is not so bad. From the look on your face I thought it was something very serious.'

'Is it not?'

'It is not exactly a laughing matter, I agree,' I said, 'but Anstruther knows his job. He has specialized somewhat in that field since I first knew him, and if he says that six weeks will help, you may rely upon him that it will.'

'But, John! Six weeks! And a two-week journey there and back. Poor Elizabeth has no-one, you know, no family or anything of that sort. She will be quite alone.'

'She has her servants, though, that married couple. And it is the tourist season, there will be plenty of people on the boat, and once she gets there.'

'Oh, servants! And strangers. What good are they? I mean no-one of her own sort, a friend. Unless she advertises for one of those horrid paid companions, some dreadful young girl who knows nothing of the world, and is sure to run off with some sheikh at the first opportunity.'

Frankly, I thought this unlikely – after all, if the girl were so dreadful and knew nothing of the world then why on earth should even an undiscriminating sheikh bother with her in the first place? – but I knew better than to say as much. 'Look here,' I said, 'why should you not go with her?'

Her face lit up at once. 'Oh, that is what I thought of at once, but I rejected the idea, of course, since it would mean leaving you alone here for such a long time.'

'Never mind about me, my darling. Of course you must accompany poor Elizabeth. You can write to me, and tell me all about it when you get back. It won't be such a very long time, after all.'

'But what will you do? I know that you won't eat properly, you'll spend all your evenings at that horrid club of yours, smoking and drinking far more than is good for you.'

I rather demurred at this slander. 'I shall be fine, ' I said. 'In point of fact, I have had a rather interesting offer, a temporary post at a very exclusive school, to help them out of a little short-term difficulty.' I thought it as well to omit any mention of Holmes's name, even under these changed circumstances. 'It will only be for a few weeks, or so I hope, so it should all work out nicely.'

On any other occasion, my wife would naturally have had a good many questions to ask about this, but so relieved was she to be able to accompany her friend that my words went almost unremarked. And indeed the prospect of her going to Egypt rather overshadowed my own little plans. We discussed the matter a little further, as it was no small step which she contemplated, but in the end we agreed that my wife should indeed go with her friend; and I am certain that you will agree that no other decision was possible.

After luncheon my wife hurried off to tell Elizabeth the news, and I strolled to the telephone. Then I had second thoughts. Holmes has sent me startling telegrams often enough, so why should I not turn the tables, give him a modest surprise? It was a fine day for January, and I had been sitting inside all morning, so I decided to combine business and pleasure. I lit my pipe, walked to the Post Office, and sent the following – 'Have decided to take up your offer of a post as English master. Can start Monday. Regards, Harold Harris.'

TWO

'And this is your room, Mr Harris.' Carstairs, the young man who acted as secretary to the Abbey School, stood aside and ushered me through the door. 'Rooms, I ought to have said,' he went on, 'for you have a study here, and a bedroom through there, quite separate. Here are your keys. If I were you, I'd keep the bedroom door locked through the day, and any personal items in there. The boys do sometimes tend to wander into the masters' studies through the day, you know. Oh, for excellent reasons, of course,' he added hastily, 'if they have to see the master concerned, or what have you. I'm not suggesting that they would pilfer anything, or anything of that kind, but they can be infernally curious, prying into things, as you doubtless know better than I.'

'But they wouldn't steal anything, surely?'

Carstairs flushed. 'I have never – that is, I have known of only one such sad occurrence in my time at the school, sir, and that was dealt with in a summary fashion. No, but boyish curiosity is not so uncommon, and it is as well to guard against it.'

'I shall take your advice, sir.'

Carstairs glanced at his watch. 'I am very sorry that Dr Longton was not here to greet you in person, but, with its being the first day of the new term, there is always a good deal to do. I am sure he will see you as soon as possible.'

'Indeed. And I shall not detain you further, sir, for I realize that you will be kept busier than most.'

Carstairs laughed, but looked relieved. 'You are right, Mr Harris. Unless I can be of any further help at the moment, I shall return to my duties. Please let me know if there is anything else you need, or if you have any questions which you think I can answer,' and he left me alone in the study.

As always, my baggage was not sizeable, and I soon distributed my things in the inner bedroom, which was commodious enough, if a trifle spartan as regards furnishings. I had brought nothing with me which might reveal my true identity, but even so I thought it might be as well to follow Carstairs's advice and keep the bedroom door locked when I was not actually occupying it. I turned the key, then, and looked round the study, which was pretty much as I seemed to remember similar rooms from my own school days, not that I saw the inside of the masters' studies much, save on those occasions – not, alas, infrequent – upon which I had to report for punishment. I shuddered at the thought, and resolved that during my tenure of office, be it never so brief, no boy in my charge should be caned, or even set the meaningless task of writing 'lines', were there any alternative humanly possible.

Just as I had taken this decision, and was wondering in a vague kind of way what to do next, there was a tap at the door, and it opened to admit a tall gentleman. 'Mr Harris?' said he. 'I am Dr Longton, sir, and I am delighted to welcome you to the Abbey School, even if it will be for only a term or so.'

Even had he not introduced himself, I would have recognized him from Holmes's description. Dr Longton was some forty years of age. He stood an inch over six feet tall, and broad in proportion, but there was not an ounce of fat on him, it was all solid muscle and bone. A glance at his face showed that he was more than simply an athlete, the strong chin, prominent nose, high forehead and shock of grey hair indicated a thinker of some calibre. The archetypal headmaster, in fact, or rather the archetype of what a headmaster ought to be, but often is not. I held out my hand. 'I am delighted to meet you, sir. Will you have a cigar?'

'And I am equally delighted to meet you.' Dr Longton's handshake was firm and manly. 'I shall not smoke, thank you, though I have no objection to your doing so at the moment. In general, though, I do not encourage the practice through the school day, or indeed after hours when it is in sight of the boys. However, should you care to come to the Senior Common Room after dinner this evening, I shall be most happy to accept your cigar, and offer you and the other masters a glass of sherry. It is our custom here to have an informal gathering of the staff on the first evening back to work, as it were.'

'You are most kind, sir.'

'Think nothing of it. I am, as I say, most gratified that you were available at such short notice.' He hesitated fractionally, or so it seemed to me. 'His Grace the Duke of Greyminster recommends you most highly, and from a cursory glance at your record, I did rather wonder why you had not been snapped up, as the vulgar phrase has it, by some rival establishment.'

'Oh, I am pretty much retired these days, and had it not been for His Grace's express request, I should never have thought about it now,' I told him. 'Indeed, I must confess that I have not had a teaching post for some ten years now, so I trust I shall not be too rusty.'

'Ah, I see. You have taught mainly in the Colonies and Dominions, as I understand?'

'In India, mostly, sir.' Holmes and I had decided upon this fiction, partly because I had been to India and thus could field any questions on the place if need be, but mainly because it would be awkward if I claimed to have been teaching at Eton, shall we say, in such and such a year, only to encounter a master who had actually been there at that time.

Dr Longton nodded, and went on, 'We have one or two Indian princes here at the moment. Possibly you will find that you are acquainted with their people?' I fervently hoped not, for most of the Indian princes I had 'met' had been looking at me over the business end of a rifle, but I did not say as much. Dr Longton shook my hand again, nodded, and said, 'If you would excuse me? The first day back, there is always plenty to occupy one's time. You know where the Third form room is?'

'Mr Carstairs showed it to me.'

'The boys will begin to arrive towards luncheon, and they will report to you there. Just tick them off the register as they give their names, and then they will go to their rooms and settle in. Any difficulties you have may be referred to Carstairs or Graves, the deputy head, or indeed to myself. And now, I must be off,' and he suited the action to the words.

I too thought it was time I buckled down to work, and so I replaced my cigar case in my pocket, with a touch of regret, and made my way to the Third form classroom. Things were quiet to begin with, then about half the boys arrived together in the late morning, I gathered that they had travelled on the same train. Another group arrived

41

after luncheon, and had to be provided with soup and sandwiches by the cooks. And finally some odd stragglers, who had missed their trains, or been driven to the school by doting parents, made their way into the classroom.

I had little to do but tick them off as they appeared. They were the usual mixed bag you get in any school, perhaps a little more confident than the ordinary run of boys, which was hardly surprising given that they came from affluent and influential families. I noticed that they regarded me with some curiosity, perhaps wondering why they had been saddled with such an old duffer – for such I must have appeared to their youthful eyes.

There were thirty-one boys in the class, which struck me as something of a coincidence, as my old school number had been thirty-one. Moreover, the boy whose name appeared on the last line of the register, beside the number '31', was none other than a Watson Minor! This double coincidence impressed me greatly; it seemed almost as if it were an omen of good luck, so if I took special notice of this youngster who had the same name as me you will not be too surprised. I turned back a page of the register, to see that there had been thirty-two boys until quite recently, the last name in the old list being that 'Whitechurch' whose dismissal had alerted Holmes to events at the school in the first place.

I noticed that Watson sat next to a boy named Edmonds, and that the two of them seemed firm friends. But I could not help but notice also that neither boy seemed entirely at ease. Now, remembering my own school days, I might have thought that it was merely an understandable reluctance to resume their studies which cast a blight over their young lives, but it seemed to me to be deeper than that. I resolved that I should ask at the first opportunity what was troubling them, and hoped that they would have sufficient confidence in me to allow me to help.

I have said that my task that day consisted of little more than ticking off the names as individuals appeared, but I had another duty, and that was to collect the cash they had brought back with them as 'pocket money', and issue each boy with a receipt. This pocket money was to be handed to Carstairs for safekeeping, and doled out at so much per week over the school term. It was a considerable amount, the average sum being far in excess of the miserable stipend I recollected from my own time at school. I was slightly taken aback by this until I recollected that these boys were from wealthy families. When the roll was complete, I told the boys to find their rooms, for I had learned that there were no communal dormitories as such, but that three or four boys shared a room. And moreover these were quite comfortable bedrooms, which I must say struck me as another quite considerable improvement on my own old school.

As I say, I had collected a large amount of money, and this was mainly in Bank of England notes and gold, there was little silver and less copper in the final total. I gathered it up and sought out Carstairs, who greeted me cheerfully. He counted the money, checked my counterfoils, and gave me another receipt for the whole. 'All businesslike, you see,' he told me.

'Yes, indeed.' I hesitated. This seemed to me to be an ideal starting point for my enquiries, and I went on, 'I confess that I was rather surprised at the magnitude of the sums involved. You must have a good deal to look after, seeing that there are seven forms, and all, presumably, handing over the same sort of amount?'

Carstairs laughed. 'Oh, there's more than seven times this amount,' he told me. 'The school has a regular sliding scale, so much per week allowed to the first-formers, and then they can have a bit more with each year's service, as it were. "Allowed" is perhaps not the right word, the school "suggests" an upper limit.'

'And the suggestion is worded so that it can't be refused?' I said.

'Just so,' said Carstairs, laughing. 'Even so, the limit is set pretty high, so the Upper Sixth live like fighting cocks on their pocket money.' He sighed, a touch enviously as it seemed to me.

'Nothing like this when I was a lad,' I said bluntly.

'Nor me, worse luck! Not that I was ever in quite this league, of course. But I was saying that there is an upper limit, and I think that's a good thing. It gives the boys an idea of what it must be like to have a set income, and a lot of them wouldn't know that without this system. When you think about it, some of these lads will never go short of anything. And some of 'em will go on to become prime ministers, judges, so they might have, quite literally, the power of life and death over their fellow men. A humbling thought.'

'It is indeed. And some of these Indian chaps, and what not –' I broke off, leaving the thought only half expressed.

Carstairs, however, seemed to sense my meaning. 'I've thought the very same thing more than once,' he said with a nod. 'In a way, we act as ambassadors for the old country. If some of these foreign potentates took it into their heads that England was less than friendly – well! Up to us to make them remember their school days as the happiest of their little lives, is it not?'

I could not help thinking that it was indeed. And with that thought a great foreboding seemed to crawl over me, like an unannounced eclipse in all the blaze and glare of full noon. What the devil was I doing here? I could not hope to fool a class of five year olds at a Board School, much less the eighteen-year-old sons of dukes, earls, bishops and maharajahs! Yes, what the devil *was* I doing here? And what the devil did Holmes mean by dragging me into his madcap schemes, particularly when I had told him I wanted nothing whatever to do with any sort of investigation, were it only as innocuous as finding a missing poodle? My one and only hope of escape, my sole chance of coming out of this hideous hash with anything approaching dignity, was to conclude the investigation as quickly as possible, and hare out of there at top speed.

I squared my shoulders, then, and nodded at the heap of cash on Carstairs's desk. 'Whatever one may think of the system, I certainly wouldn't care for the responsibility of looking after that sort of pile of cash. Just glad it's out of my hands now.'

'Oh,' said Carstairs carelessly, 'I don't have the worry of looking after it, thank the Lord. I'll turn it over to the head, and he'll put it in his safe until tomorrow, when I shall take it to the bank. Then I go back to the bank to draw out the appropriate amount each Thursday or Friday, the head locks that away again until I ask him for it, then I hand it to you chaps, who dole it out on Friday night or Saturday morning, as seems best to you. All very safe and secure.'

'Unless someone hits you on the head on the way to or from the bank?' I suggested.

Carstairs laughed. 'I vary the day and time that I go, a bit, so that there's no set pattern a crook could spot. And the school caretaker goes with me. I don't know if you've met him, but he's an ex-prizefighter, and pretty rough and tough. We haven't had any trouble thus far.'

'Glad to hear it.' I hesitated, as if reluctant to bring the topic up. 'Although didn't someone tell me that a boy had taken some money from Dr Longton's study last term?'

'Who told you that?' asked Carstairs quickly.

'I don't know if I recall who it was,' said I, being deliberately vague. 'You know how it is when you're thinking of taking up a post at a new school, you ask questions, take notice of what is being said about the place. You yourself mentioned something of the sort earlier, for that matter."

'Yes, of course,' said Carstairs with something like relief. 'I trust it was me – I – who told you, for I wouldn't like to think that the tale is being bandied about generally outside the school. Well, whoever it may have been, they had it right, for there was an unfortunate incident towards the end of last term. But we don't like to talk about it, you know.'

'Indeed not. But if one of the boys in one's charge were to be that way inclined, it might be as well to know about it, don't you think? Only fair, and all that.'

'The boy in question was expelled, sir.' There was an odd note in Carstairs's voice. Did he not believe what he said, or was he merely desirous of changing the subject, I wondered.

I raised an eyebrow. 'You do not sound wholeheartedly convinced, Mr Carstairs.'

He glanced at the door of his room, which was closed, and lowered his voice. 'I know the boy's family, sir, and it struck me as being very strange indeed. Positively fishy, in fact. You will, I am sure, hear talk, rumours, during your time here, so it might be as well to know the truth. The boy accused of the theft was young Lord Whitechurch, son of the Duke of Greyminster.'

'Good Lord!' I feigned surprise at this. 'But the duke is one of the richest men in all England, is he not?'

'In the world, more like,' nodded Carstairs. 'And the amount he was accused of taking was twenty-five pounds. Oh, for most folk that is a hefty sum, even you or I would not dismiss it lightly, but for the Duke of Greyminster, and for Lord Whitechurch, it is a trifle. If the boy had needed that amount, he could have telegraphed to his father. Or he could have used what we call our little "imprest" system, that is to say he could have borrowed against this next term's pocket money. No, it is very curious that he should have wanted, or needed, to take that sum. And that is not the only curious aspect of the matter, nor the most curious aspect of it either.'

'No?'

'No, sir.' Carstairs glanced again at the door that led to the corridor, then nodded at the other door on the far side of his study, which led, I took it, to Dr Longton's room. 'Dr Longton is not in his study at the moment,' he said, confirming my guess, 'and obviously I should not be gossiping like this if he were. And equally obviously, I rely upon you, sir, not to discuss the matter further.'

'Oh, of course.'

'But that door, although closed, is not locked,' Carstairs went on, again indicating the door to the head's study. 'If I needed something from Dr Longton's room, a ledger, a file, even a stamp, were I to run out of them, I should simply go in there and take what I needed. Of course, if the head were in his room, I should knock first, and wait until given leave to enter.'

I raised an eyebrow. 'A touch informal?'

'Dr Longton is not starchy, sir.'

'No, I meant rather that anyone could go in there. After all, you wouldn't want a boy looking at his own file or what have you, would you? Or a master, come to that.'

Carstairs laughed. 'The files and books are locked away safely, sir. Dr Longton has one set of keys, I have another, and nobody else can get at the private documents. That was the point I was about to make. Two points, really. One being that although anyone could, in theory, get into his study quite easily, Dr Longton is the most scrupulous of men when it comes to locking away valuables. The other, although perhaps it is, strictly speaking, an amplification or demonstration of the first point, is that I myself have been in and out of his study – what? – a dozen times a day for the last couple of years, and never have I seen money left out in plain view. Never. You see now why I find it well-nigh incredible that bank notes should have been left reposing on his desk. And then there is the whole question of a boy's actually daring to go into the headmaster's room at all. The usual course would be for the boy to report to me, and for me to inform the head that a boy wished to see him.'

'And if you were not in here for some reason?'

'The boy would simply wait until I arrived,' said Carstairs.

'So you are sometimes out of the room?'

'I pop in and out all the time. But even I do not know just when I shall be popping out, so how could a boy possibly know? Oh, I grant you that a boy might come in here and find that I was out, but he would not dare to disturb the headmaster. He would sit quietly over there,' and Carstairs pointed to a couple of wicker chairs that stood against the far wall, 'until I returned.'

'And suppose this hypothetical boy had seen you leave, seen the head outside somewhere, and thus knew that he had a few moments until one or both of you should return?' I asked.

Carstairs shook his head. 'It is possible, though improbable. But granted that the improbable had occurred, we then come across the other objection, namely that the money should not have been left out in the first place.'

'Dr Longton may have just taken it from his safe, though? Or have been about to place it in the safe? He may have been called away unexpectedly?'

'I can recall no sort of emergency upon the day in question,' said Carstairs shortly. 'And in any event, if some emergency did chance to prevent one locking the notes away a drawer or filing cabinet, would the logical course of action not be to put them in one's pocket? I cannot understand why the head simply left them lying about like that. Most uncharacteristic.'

'H'mm. I suppose they were just lying about, though? No chance of anyone taking them out of the safe?'

Carstairs shook his head. 'Even I don't have a key to the safe. There are two of them, the head has one on his watch chain, the other is held by the chairman of the school governors, himself a wealthy man in his own right, and a JP to boot. Nothing there, I'm afraid.'

'No, I see that.'

'And then they were Bank of England notes, five notes of five pounds each, and brand new. Everyone knows that such notes can be traced readily enough by their numbers. It makes no sense at all.'

'I wonder why the money was there in the first place?'

'I have said that money goes in and out each week,' said

Carstairs. 'As a matter of strict, accurate fact, I myself had handed that week's cash over to the head that same morning, so I assume the notes were part of that.'

'Well, that explains that. As to the oddity of the matter, you have quite convinced me,' I told him. 'But its being odd hardly solves the puzzle. After all, one must ask a further question. If this lad did not steal the notes, then who did?'

Carstairs shrugged his shoulders. 'I have asked myself that question, and more than once or twice, Mr Harris, you may be sure. Had the boy not been seen leaving the head's room, or the notes not been found amongst his possessions, the logical suspect would have been yours truly, and that might have proved a touch awkward for me.' He produced a silk handerchief and wiped his brow before going on, 'And if I had actually done it – well! Instant dismissal, and ruin, for one would never get another post in the profession.'

'Indeed not. Who saw the boy, by the way? You?'

Carstairs shook his head. 'The first I knew about it was at morning assembly, just like the rest of them. That was another odd thing; you'd think the head would've mentioned it to me and the other staff first.'

'Well, it is something of a puzzle. And I understand that there was a second upset of a more serious sort towards the end of last term?'

'Ah, yes.' Carstairs looked embarrassed at this.

'Again, it might be as well if I knew the facts,' I pointed out, 'rather than hearing all sorts of wretched stories and rumours –' I broke off as the door opened, and a short but bulky man, with dark hair and extremely bushy eyebrows, entered the room.

THREE

The newcomer glanced at me with some considerable distaste, and I realized that I had unconsciously assumed a relaxed attitude and was half sitting on the edge of Carstairs's desk. I levered myself to my feet, and nodded a greeting to the man who had just entered the room.

Carstairs hurriedly stood up and said, 'Mr Graves, this is Mr Harris, the new English master. Mr Harris, this is the deputy head, Mr Graves.'

'Delighted, sir!' said I, holding out my hand.

Graves looked as if he would have liked to ignore my overture, but then took hold of my hand for long enough to give it a perfunctory shake, mumbling something or the other which I could not catch as he did so. He turned at once to Carstairs. 'I have merely come to hand over the Upper Sixth's pocket money,' and he heaped a great pile of gold and notes upon the table.

'Just being doing the same. Rather like the Sunday collection in church, is it not?' I said, attempting to invest the situation with a suggestion of humour.

Graves evidently did not see the joke. He cast me a single withering glance, then told Carstairs, 'I should be grateful for the usual receipt.' When Carstairs had hastily counted the cash and issued a chit for it, Graves went on to me, 'I am sure Mr Carstairs has much to do on the first day of term, so perhaps we should leave him undisturbed?'

I took the hint readily enough. I nodded to Carstairs, and followed Graves out of the room.

'You must not blame Mr Carstairs for being temporarily distracted from his duties, you know,' I told Graves as we strolled down the corridor. 'I'm afraid I was asking him a good many questions about the school, and I am sure you will understand my thirst for knowledge.'

Graves stopped, turned, and looked at me. 'You do not know our little ways, Mr Harris,' said he, 'but the fact is that many of us, the masters, that is to say, have been at this school for the whole of our working lives. In fact many of us were pupils here. I was myself. And whilst we do not like to think of ourselves as stuffy, or backward looking, we do rather tend to have our little hierarchy. The senior masters do not, as a rule, associate too much with the younger men, such as Mr Carstairs.' He gazed at me with wonderfully penetrating eyes from under those bushy brows.

'Of course,' I said. 'I quite understand. But then I myself am something of a new boy, so to speak. Not in years, of course – would that I were! But in terms of experience. Of the Abbey School, that is to say,' I added hastily, lest he think I was meaning my teaching career generally. 'So obviously I have a lot to learn, and I really need to know my way about the place as quickly as possible, if I am to fit in halfway through the year, as it were, without too much disruption.'

Graves seemed to soften somewhat at this. 'Yes, yes, I can see that.'

'In point of fact, I was rather hoping to persuade Carstairs, or someone else, to act as an unofficial guide, show me round the school.'

'And perhaps tell you a little of our history?'

There was a curious note in Graves's voice, keenness blended with a hint of diffidence, perhaps? I glanced at him, and seemed to see in his eyes reflections of those perished cities whose great phantasmata o'erbrow the silent citizens of this or that. I was prompted to ask him, 'You are yourself something of an expert in the history of the school, perhaps, sir?'

He smiled, positively eager to respond. 'An amateur, sir, nothing more. History is my subject, you see, and also by way of a hobby of sorts. I think I may say without boasting that no man knows more of the history of the Abbey School than I do.' He looked at the oak panelling of the corridor, the pictures of what I took to be former pupils on the walls, the stained glass that still shone out in the slanting rays of the winter sun. 'I love this old place, you know,' he said, quite unexpectedly. 'I have been here pretty well all my life.'

'In that case, sir, I should consider it an honour if you could find the time to show me around,' I said. 'Whenever it may chance to be convenient to you, that is.'

Graves consulted his watch. 'We have some time before the dinner bell, so if you are free at the moment? Yes? I can do no more than scratch the surface, you understand, in so short a time, and particularly as it grows dark, but it may serve to whet your appetite.'

He led me down the corridor, pausing to indicate a particularly fine portrait here and there, and then took me through the assembly hall to the main door. 'You get a better overall view of the school from the other end of the drive,' said Graves, setting off at a fair pace. I made what speed I could, but I had all on to keep up with Graves, who glanced back after a score of paces, and asked, 'Do you have trouble with your leg, sir?'

'I do,' I answered. 'A souvenir of India, I fear.'

Graves slowed down. 'Ah, I beg your pardon. My eagerness to show the place off outweighed my courtesy.' He looked at me again. 'You are too young to have fought in the Mutiny, so I guess the Afghan campaign?' He raised his bushy eyebrows.

'Absolutely correct,' I told him.

'It must have been most interesting. You must tell us all about it some time.'

Not likely, was the vulgar retort which came to my mind. In fact I cursed myself silently for having given even that much away. Still, I had already claimed that all my teaching experience was in India, so perhaps no great harm had been done. I smiled weakly, and walked on in silence.

'Now,' said Graves, as we reached the porter's little lodge at the main gate. 'How's that for a prospect?'

When I had arrived at the school that morning I had been riding in a cab which I found at the station, and through the window, obscured with condensation, I had not been able to see much more than the trees in the driveway, so this was my first real look at the building. It was a lovely sight that met my eyes. The setting sun lit up the mellow grey stone and the slates all covered with lichen, and made the stained glass windows glow as if lamps had been lit behind them.

The school buildings themselves were extensive. The tower from which the unfortunate young man had fallen, if fallen he had, lay straight ahead of us at the end of the carriage drive, and dominated the whole view. It was some eighty feet high, and had something of the appearance of a clock tower or bell tower in a church.

Below this tower was the outer door of heavy oak, through which we had just come. Through that door was a short passage, actually built into, and part of, the base of the tower. This passage led to an inner door which gave on to the assembly hall.

The main body of the building, three storeys high, ran to left and right of the tower and the great outer door, and ran for a considerable distance, too. I knew that on the far side of the building, hidden from my sight at the moment, were short wings at right angles to the main block. These were mostly used by servants, or as store rooms, I gathered. Then a stable block at which ran parallel to the main building at the rear had been partly converted to house modern chemical laboratories and the like, and formed the fourth side of the quadrangle.

'Proper country house,' I remarked.

Graves nodded. 'It was built as such three hundred years ago.'

'Where's the abbey, then? Or wasn't there one?'

'There was, centuries ago. The records are fragmentary, I regret to say, but there was certainly a foundation here by 1155. The earliest mention I have found is of one Abbot Roger de Jourdain, or Jordan, a determined man but a fair one by all accounts, a man who kept his unruly monks in order with an iron hand. No easy task, I gather. The abbey did not survive the Dissolution, and the land was sold to a local gentleman who built the present house, or at least the older part of it, for his descendants added to it quite considerably.'

'I thought the tower looked early eighteenth century.'

Graves nodded. 'It is. Perhaps the owner at that time thought it gave the house something of an ecclesiastical look not entirely inappropriate to its origins? Or perhaps it was merely one of those "follies" which were popular at that time?' Somewhat hurriedly, as if he wanted to change the subject, he said, 'The ruins of the abbey are still here, by the way.'

'Oh?'

'Yes. I believe that some of the stones were incorporated into the house. And some of the stained glass, although much of it is comparatively new, as you will doubtless have observed. Again the owner of the day seems to have thought stained glass suitable for a house with such a beginning.'

'The house was not built directly upon the old foundations of the abbey, then?' I asked.

'No, the ruins are over there,' and Graves swung round to indicate a point to the far left of the school grounds. 'In that little spinney affair.'

I gazed at the little knot of trees on the edge of the grass sward. 'Must be quite interesting. I think I may take a stroll over there when I have an hour or so to spare.'

Graves frowned. 'There is not much to see, the place is quite ruinous. Although there is an underground room which is not entirely devoid of all interest. I may add that the ruins are out of bounds to the boys, although it is sometimes difficult to ensure that they keep out. And masters are requested –' and he stressed the 'requested' rather significantly – 'not to go clambering about there and setting a bad example to the lads. I myself have conducted a survey of the place, but that was some time ago, and conducted under strictly scientific conditions, of course. I made some flashlight photographs, which I shall be more than pleased to show you.'

'Of course I shall not dream of going there, if that is the correct form,' I said at once. But privately I thought, Oh, yes? An underground chamber in a ruined abbey, out of bounds to all and sundry? Surely if there were anything untoward happening, that was the very place for it? I resolved to explore the ruins at the earliest opportunity. Seeking to change the subject, I asked, 'If it was first an abbey, and next a private house, when did the school come along?'

'It is an interesting question. The records, as I say, are exiguous in the extreme, but I have found a hint that there was a school associated with the abbey from the very earliest times. Not an uncommon occurrence, of course, particularly where there were choristers. If there were indeed a school in those early days, then like the abbey itself it vanished at the Dissolution. The present establishment dates from the beginning of this century.'

'I see.'

We stood there in silence for five minutes or so, then Graves suddenly shivered. 'It seems to have turned colder.'

'Sun's gone now,' I said. 'A fire and a glass of something warming might be rather pleasant.'

Graves laughed. 'I concur, sir. The normal practice here is to wait until after dinner, at which nothing stronger than tea is served. Then, of course, masters may drink what they will in the Senior Common Room, provided always that no bad example is set to the boys.'

'Of course that is understood. But I am relieved to find that you are not all teetotallers here,' I said. Which was nothing more or less than the truth, I may add.

'Oh, by no means. Within reason, that is to say. Did the Greek philosopher not counsel "moderation in all things"?'

'I thought it was "all things in moderation", you know.'

'A common misapprehension, sir.' Graves started back towards the school building. As we hurried along, for it had turned quite cold by this time, he added, 'As it is the first day of term, though, we might stretch a point, do you think? Since there is a nip in the air outside, we might indulge in a "nip" indoors?' He compensated for this atrocious pun by adding, 'I have a rather superior oloroso, if you have a few moments to spare?'

I agreed readily enough, and went with Graves to his study. His sherry was excellent, its age complementing the sweetness, and I accepted a second glass. 'Mustn't overdo it, though,' I said.

'Indeed not.'

It now occurred to me that I had pretty well covered all the ground that I could with regard to Lord Whitechurch's expulsion, and I might just as well take this opportunity to ask some pertinent questions about the other, more serious, matter. 'I have often thought that this is one of the greatest dangers facing men such as ourselves,' I added, raising my glass. 'A hard day's teaching, a roaring fire, the temptation to have a second glass.'

Graves sighed. 'We've all seen it, have we not? Not so much here, thank Heaven.'

'Oh? I thought I had heard some talk of the young man whom I replaced?'

Graves set down his glass on the table. He sighed again, more theatrically this time. 'People will gossip so, you know.'

'Understandable, when you consider the rather singular circumstances under which I obtained this post.' And I repeated what I had said to Carstairs, 'Better to hear the true facts from an authoritative source such as yourself, than overhear silly rumours from the boys. For they are sure to talk about it in my presence sooner or later.'

'H'mm, I suppose so. Well, the general consensus seems to

be that he drank himself silly, then climbed the tower and either threw himself off deliberately, or else lost his footing by sheer accident.'

'Do you share in the general consensus?'

Graves frowned. 'It was a very curious affair, I must say. The young man had been here a couple of years, and as deputy head I very naturally took him under my wing to some extent, took particular notice of his abilities and so forth. Certainly I never saw him drunk, nor even slightly tipsy. Of course,' he added doubtfully, 'one hears of secret drinkers, and so on. But I'd never have believed it of young Greville. Again, how did he get into the tower? The only ingress is via the little door in the passageway between the inner and outer doors, and that is normally kept locked, for obvious reasons.' He frowned, and added, 'Although it was not locked that morning.'

'And the key?'

'The headmaster has one, I think, and the porter certainly has another.'

'Now, that *is* curious. Was any key found on the young man's body, do you recall?'

Graves shot me a look. 'Is there some reason for the question, sir?'

'Oh, just idle curiosity. Well, possibly more than that, you know. In India, of course, as an Englishman, I often had to look into little problems for the locals. It was expected that one would possess the judgement of Solomon.' Rather neat, that, I thought.

'I see. And, in point of fact, I have mused about that myself. No, sir, he had no key about his person. The accepted theory is that the porter had unlocked the door in connection with his duties, and forgotten to lock it again after him.

There is nothing in the tower, of course, it is not even used as a store room, but the porter occasionally goes in there to check the roof, after a storm, shall we say, or to make sure that the glass in the windows is sound.'

'And had he been in there about the time that the young man died?'

'The porter had been up there about a week previously, and replaced a pane of glass broken in the autumn gales. He swore that he had locked the door afterwards, of course. But it was indubitably unlocked on the morning that the body was found.'

'And had this porter left doors unlocked, or anything of that kind, before then?'

Graves frowned. 'He has occasionally had a slight lapse of memory. I am sure most of us would have to admit the same.'

'Oh, indeed. Still, it is a rather odd chain of coincidences, is it not?'

Graves looked at me intently for a while before he spoke. 'What exactly are you suggesting, Mr Harris?'

'Oh, I'm not suggesting anything,' I told him quickly. 'Just an odd chain of circumstances, that's all. The young man was unused to drink, he had one too many, found the door open – yes, I can see how it might happen. Tell me, I did not particularly notice the tower as we returned to the school, but is it open at the top, is there a door or something? How did he actually get out?'

'There is a window at the very top, big enough for a man to climb through without any great difficulty.'

'But he would have to climb through the window? There is no door, or anything like that? He could not just have fallen?'

'He would have had to make up his mind to climb out,

yes.'

'I see. Dreadful business.'

'Indeed.' Almost as if he were conscious of having said too much and wanted to change the subject, Graves rose from his chair and went to a cupboard. 'I promised to show you those photographs of the ruins, I think? If you are interested, that is.' He brought a leather album over to the table.

'I should be more than interested,' I said, truthfully enough.

Graves was evidently a skilled photographer, and I studied the pictures intently. The ruins left above ground were neither extensive nor particularly attractive, but there were a couple of plates, evidently taken with the aid of magnesium powder, of the underground room which Graves had mentioned. It was much bigger than I had expected, with a proper vaulted ceiling, rather like the nave of a cathedral, though on a smaller scale. A shallow flight of steps led upwards, evidently to an entrance at ground level, and there were three or four large stone pillars to support the ceiling. 'Impressive,' I said. 'What would that have been used for, do you think?'

Graves shrugged his shoulders. 'Hard to say. It may have been nothing more than a store room of some sort. Even barns of the day were impressive structures. Of course, the boys have all sorts of different explanations,' he added with a laugh.

'Secret societies, wicked monks, and that sort of thing? Yes, I expect they have.' I indicated the stairs shown in the picture. 'These lead to the entrance at ground level, I suppose?'

'Yes, there is a door, not original, but placed there later. It is kept locked, for, as I told you, we discourage visitors.'

'Oh? Are you quite sure it's locked? The tower door was open, I believe you said.'

'I checked the door in the ruins, the day of the tragedy. You may be sure of that,' said Graves with some emphasis.

'And who has that key? You?'

'The headmaster keeps that key as well. If you are genuinely interested, I can try to arrange a visit. I would be more than pleased to show you round, and it will be much safer, as I know the place. The masonry is a little insecure in places, a natural consequence of the passage of time.'

'It is extremely kind of you to offer, sir, and I assure you I should be most interested,' I told him. I looked at the clock. 'I must not detain you any longer just at the moment, though, as we shall have to think about getting ready for dinner.'

'Indeed.' Graves shook my hand in a most friendly manner, and on that happy note I took my leave.

Unsurprisingly, when you consider the age and size of the school buildings, there were a good many doors leading out into the quadrangle. Graves's rooms were near one of these doors. And my own rooms were quite near yet another of them, but were at some distance from Graves's rooms, if I make myself clear. It seemed to me that it would be much easier for me to return to my rooms by going outside and across the quadrangle, particularly considering that I did not yet properly know my way round the maze of corridors and rooms.

I let myself out, then, and hurried across the stone flags, now damp with a thin wintry drizzle. It was much colder than it had been earlier, and I lowered my head against a stiff breeze, eager to get back to my own rooms, light the fire, if that had not already been done, and get tidied up ready for dinner.

I have said that I lowered my head, and thus I did not notice another man who was crossing the quadrangle but in the opposite direction to me. Not, that is, until we all but collided, for he too was walking head down, bracing himself against the heavy weather.

'I beg your pardon, sir,' said I, pulling myself up just in time to prevent myself knocking him over, for he was a tall, thin, elderly man.

'Not a bit of it, sir! Entirely my fault. I was not looking where I was going, I fear. I was musing, to be plain, upon the austere beauty of the imaginary numbers.'

'Oh? And what are they when they're at home, then? Sounds like my bank balance. Or perhaps my tailor's bills.'

He blinked at me as the rain struck his face. 'They are, as every schoolboy knows, the numbers which have as a component the square root of minus one.'

I wrinkled my brow. 'I can't remember much about it,' I confessed, 'but I seem to recollect that minus one cannot have a square root.'

'No more it can, sir, no more it can! Of course it cannot. Ridiculous to suppose that it could. But imagine for one moment, if you will, that it could. Ah, there's the mystery and the beauty of it! In that imagination is all the challenge, the riddle, and – yes, I shall say it, plainly and unashamedly – the sheer fun!' He scrabbled in the pocket of a rusty frock coat. 'Mathematics is my field, sir, and that is my card.'

'Ah. I fear I have no cards just at present,' I said, embarrassed. 'Just taken this post, you know, and had no time to get them printed.' This was partly true; although part of the reason was that I hoped to conclude my investigations before I had many social engagements to perform. 'Harris is the name, sir. Pleased to meet you.'

He shook my hand in an absent-minded sort of way, and started back the way he had come. 'You were going the other way, surely, sir?' I told him. 'I was going this way.'

'Oh? Yes, to be sure. Of course, if the distance be not infinite, then logically one should come back to the same spot.'

'But not in time for dinner.'

He stared at me. 'An interesting premise, sir. We shall meet again, I have no doubt.' And off he went, in the right direction this time.

I found my own rooms, and was pleased to see that one of the servants had lit a decent fire. I removed my coat, glanced at the card the old fellow had given me – 'James I Tromarty,' it read – and then got ready for dinner. This was held in a dining hall quite separate from the main hall, with masters and boys all dining together, and it was preceded by another roll call in the classroom. My thirty-one charges were all settled in, and somewhat inclined to be boisterous, a circumstance I attributed to the beginning of the new term, and the proximity to dinner.

At dinner Graves was naturally seated next to Dr Longton, and the only other man I had met so far, the old chap I had bumped into in the quad, whose name I had forgotten, was down the other end of the table, so I found myself seated between two men I had not met hitherto. On my right was a short, round, balding, elderly man named Donaldson, who taught music, and on my left Herr Wieland, the German master, thirty-odd years old, with startlingly blue eyes, blond hair and the strapping physique of the mountaineer.

Mr Donaldson proved to be a trifle deaf, and his conversation was largely centred upon his chosen subject. He told me at great length about the eighteenth-century organ, now in sad disrepair and pretty well walled up at one end of the assembly hall, and his unassuming ambition to restore it to its former glory that it might peal out of a morning to the glory of God and the greater honour of the school. Having spoken on this topic, as I say, for some time, he appeared to fall asleep, and I got into conversation with Herr Wieland. As I had suspected, he was a great one for climbing and walking in the hills, and something of a huntsman to boot, as are many of his compatriots. We thus had much in common, and I impressed him with some yarns about my time in India, being careful, however, not to give too much away which might hint at my true identity.

We touched briefly on politics, though I could not tell you how we got on to that subject; perhaps it was the mention of India that did it. Herr Wieland was very hot on the subject of German expansion. 'Britain has her empire, Russia hers, France her colonies. Germany, too, is a world-class power, and she will not be confined to her present boundaries for ever,' he told me confidently.

'You have your own colonies in Africa,' I pointed out.

'Pah!' He dismissed this with a contemptuous gesture worthy of any Junker. 'It is a start, I grant you, but it will not be enough in the future.'

I had no great desire to get into an argument on my first day, so I changed the subject, and shortly after the meal came to a close. The boys filed off, and the masters followed Dr Longton to the Senior Common Room, for the promised glass of sherry, which was, I may say, by no means of the same quality as Graves's had been, but was very drinkable none the less.

I was now introduced to such of the masters as I had not yet met. I shall give you their names, though I do not for one moment expect you to remember them, any more than I did, at least at that time, for they seemed to me to march towards me in a continuous procession, and I barely had time to shake hands and murmur, 'How d'you do?' before the next one arrived. There was Monsieur Legrand, the French master; Mr Dennison, geography; Mr Reed, sciences; and Mr Huxtable, classics.

This last name rang a bell with me. 'Mr Huxtable?' I asked him. 'You are not by any chance related to Dr Huxtable of the Priory School, the author of *Huxtable's Sidelights on Horace*, are you?'

He glowered at me. 'My brother, sir.'

Oh, Lord, I thought, for I had met Dr Huxtable a year or so previous to this on a case I had investigated with Holmes, and I dreaded the thought that my identity might be revealed as a consequence. I became aware that Mr Huxtable was speaking to me.

'Do you know my brother, sir?'

'I can scarcely claim any acquaintance,' I temporized, 'but his fame is quite considerable.'

'Indeed it is! Are you aware, sir, that I myself did a considerable amount of the research on the work you mentioned?'

'Ah – no. Can't say I am.'

'Yes, sir. And not one word of credit was I given! Not one, sir. For which reason, and because there is some natural rivalry between the two establishments, I have not, unbrotherly though it may seem to you, I have not spoken to my brother this last ten years, sir, nor he to me.'

Thank Heaven for that, I told myself with a sigh of relief. Considerably reassured, I gave Mr Huxtable a broad grin, and shook his hand heartily a second time, which seemed to surprise him slightly.

I may add here that seven of the masters had charge of a form. Dr Longton, as head, did not, and nor did old Mr Donaldson, who looked too frail to keep order among a meadow full of butterflies, nor Mr Reed, the science master, who was only twenty-five or so, was recently married, and who lived in the village, about three-quarters of a mile away. Mr Reed left the gathering early, to go home.

Carstairs, the school secretary, was present, and the matron, a Miss Windlass, looked in for five minutes at the end of our little gathering. Miss Windlass was a lady of around forty years of age, strikingly handsome, but with a nononsense air about her. I presume this was essential, as she was about the only woman, other than the cooks and maids, all elderly and respectable, with whom the boys and masters had any dealings.

All in all, the gathering passed pleasantly enough, but I was not too sorry when it was over and we took our leave of Dr Longton. It had been one of the longest days of my life, and quite frankly I wondered if I should be able to stand the pace. And yet I had done nothing, or nothing that I could put a name to, apart from supervise a classroom full of young boys! Perhaps, I thought as I sought my bed, both Holmes and I had underestimated the difficulties of the teacher's life?

FOUR ·

'**W**atson! Watson!' It was Holmes's voice, rousing me from my sleep. I tried to sit up, but had a considerable struggle with the bedclothes, which seemed to have taken on a life of their own.

'Holmes, is that you? What on earth are you doing here?'

'You called me in, to help you out, do you not remember? But there is no time for explanations now. You must take command of your section and go to Maiwand, for there is trouble there.'

'Trouble? At Maiwand?' Try as I might, I could not understand him. 'And what do you mean by my section?'

'Why, the Conic section, of course. Quick, man, the Surds have rebelled, and only you can save the Empire!'

I struggled for a suitable reply, but, 'I'd have said you're the Surd, Holmes, bursting into my dreams like this,' was the best I could manage.

'Come, Watson, the game is afoot! The Professor has calculated the dynamics of an asteroid to the nth degree, and he will send it spinning into the sun with disastrous consequences to the ecliptic if you do not prevent it!'

'The Professor? Which professor do you mean, Holmes?'

'Why, Moriarty, of course. Is there more than one professor, Watson? Only you know him better as Mr Tromarty, I fancy.'

'Tromarty? Of course, Holmes! I knew that name rang a bell – rang a bell – a bell –'

It was then that I woke. I was drenched with perspiration, despite its being the second week in January, and I had got the bedclothes wrapped round my neck, so that I must have resembled a woodcut illustration of the Ancient Mariner with that damned albatross.

I sat up in bed, aware that the bell that had somehow got into my dreams – though I could not recall the details just then – was the alarm clock on the bedside table. I reached out, for it was pitch black, found the clock and silenced it.

Then I got the blankets into some sort of order, and sat there shivering. I fumbled around on the bedside table until I found a match. I lit it, found a candle and lit that. The light dispersed the last of my fears, and I laughed to myself. 'A bad dream, that's all. Can't quite recollect what it was all about.' Holmes, I remembered that, but something more, something Holmes had been trying to tell me. What the devil had it been?

I looked at the clock. I am not one of nature's early risers, nor a particularly consistent riser, as a rule, but I had not wanted to get a reputation as a sluggard during my time at the Abbey School, and so I had bought the loudest alarm clock they had in the shop. I had also taken the precaution of setting it twenty minutes ahead of the time I meant to rise on this first real day of duty, so that I might be able either to get up early, or – and this struck me as the more likely possibility – to turn over for another twenty minutes. I therefore had time to do a little hard thinking.

Holmes, he was part of my dream, yes. And trying desperately to warn me about something. Or someone? I felt that I was getting closer, but I knew that if I tried to recapture my thoughts of the night I should merely succeed in driving them away altogether. I must approach the problem obliquely.

Now, I am not a great believer in the supernatural, or thought transference, or anything of that kind, so I dismissed at once the notion that Holmes himself had, in some uncanny fashion, been trying to warn me of something. The message, whatever it may have been, had come from my own mind, that 'unconscious' or 'subconscious' mind that was currently provoking so much debate amongst certain of my medical colleagues. I recalled hearing a lecture a year or so back by one very eminent professor –

Of course! That had broken my dream. Professor Moriarty, to be sure. And Mr Tromarty. That was it. Just a silly dream. But was there nothing more to it than just a silly dream? Could Tromarty possibly be Moriarty? I frowned. I got out of bed, and hurried to my little wardrobe. I found the visiting card which Mr Tromarty had given me the previous evening, a scrap of paper and a stub of pencil.

Now for the acid test. 'James I Tromarty.' I wrote it out on my bit of paper, crossed out letters here and there, and stared in horror at the end result. It could not possibly be true! I checked again, and again, only the third time I worked backwards, so to speak. It rang true every time: 'James I Tromarty' was a perfect anagram of 'James T Moriarty'!

Wait, though, wait, wait, wait, I mumbled to myself. It was too perfect, too pat, too obvious. And by a very long chalk. The real Moriarty was nobody's fool, he would never employ so crude a device. 'Was' nobody's fool, and 'would' never employ it? I laughed. Moriarty was dead, had been these ten years and more!

I glanced at the clock again. Ten minutes before the time I had appointed as my hour of rising. Well, I could turn over, for those ten minutes. Or a quarter of an hour, perhaps? That would mean I was only five minutes later getting up than I had intended, after all, and ever since my army days I have always been able to dress and shave quicker than most men.

I blew out the candle, and snuggled into the bed. Funny the tricks the mind can play! One old mathematics teacher, a curious coincidence of names, together with the investigation I was engaged upon, these were the things which had kindled my imagination. Would that it could work so well, and with so little solid basis for inspiration, when I sat before those blank sheets of foolscap! No, it was nonsense, all nonsense. Moriarty was dead. Dead at Reichenbach. Dead these last ten years or more.

But what about his brothers? I sat up in bed yet again. I knew that Professor James Moriarty, mathematics expert and criminal genius, had two brothers. One was, or had been, a colonel in the army, and the other was – what? I struggled to recall. A bus conductor, or train driver or something of that sort, was it? No, a station master. That was it, a station master. And I knew that the colonel, at any rate, had also had the name 'James', for I remember that it struck me as odd. A family name, possibly, I thought now, or the mother's maiden name? Perhaps the 'T' of my anagram, which I had thought was the middle initial, was in fact the first name, 'T James Moriarty'?

This quibbling over nomenclature was not germane to my immediate purpose. Names or brothers be what they may, the same old objection applied. Too damned easy. Even if Moriarty's brothers were both of the same evil persuasion, and it was by no means certain that they were, for there had never been any suggestion of that sort, but supposing for a moment that they were inclined to evil, and supposing that they had their brother's flair for mathematics, and further supposing that Mr Tromarty was one of those brothers, then he would presumably have sufficient wit to hide his identity in a halfway decent fashion?

On the other hand, would a complicated alias be necessary? Professor Moriarty had never come to trial, so his name had not been blazoned about the popular press in the same way as the name of, say, Colonel Moran, who was Moriarty's trusted henchman. It is true that Professor Moriarty's brother, Colonel James Moriarty, had attempted to blacken the name of my friend Sherlock Holmes a few years after the supposed death of Holmes and the actual death of the professor, by writing some absurd letters to the newspapers. And as a consequence I had been obliged to set out the true facts in the story which I called *The Final Problem*. But that was printed in, what, 1893? Ten years ago, or thereabouts, at any rate. Long enough for the average reader to have pretty well forgotten all about Professor Moriarty. Add to that the fact that the masters at an exclusive establishment like the Abbey School had probably never even seen a copy of anything so workaday as the *Strand* magazine; add the further fact that anyone who had read my account must know that Professor Moriarty was dead, and the need for elaborate disguise surely vanished?

In any event, here was a second curious factor. The first was the old ruined abbey, out of bounds to all and sundry, and this Mr Tromarty was the second. It looked as if I had both my man and my site marked down, and I had not been at the school a full twenty-four hours! Holmes himself could scarcely have done better. Well, I now had two definite objects. The first was to become better acquainted with the mysterious Mr Tromarty, and the second was to explore those ruins.

First, however, I had a day's teaching to put in. I had been rather dreading it, but now it seemed to pale into insignificance beside my two major discoveries. After all, if I could solve the problem quickly, I should soon be waving a none-too-fond farewell to the Abbey School. Fired by this thought, I got up and was very soon washed and dressed.

The preliminaries to the day's work, roll call, breakfast, assembly, passed quickly and easily enough, and at nine o'clock I stood in front of my first class. As good luck would have it, this maiden effort was with 'my own' class, the Third, so at any rate I did not have to face a room full of curious strangers. I had been told that Dr Longton had taken charge of the Third on a temporary basis for the last couple of weeks of the old term, and his final instructions to the boys had been to write a lengthy composition during the Christmas break on the topic, 'How I would spend the ideal holiday'. This, to be blunt, struck me as a pretty mean thing to saddle the poor boys with, but they had all obeyed the instructions, and now solemnly passed their sheets of foolscap along the rows and up to me, so that I soon had an impressive pile on the desk before me.

I confess that my heart sank at the prospect of reading through these essays; from my earliest days as a writer I have been familiar with the phenomenon to which I append the long-winded but perfectly accurate label, 'I have always thought that I could write, if only . . .' with the sentence being variously ended, if only the speaker did not have to take the family on holiday to Southsea, or oversee the killing of the Christmas goose, or dig the vegetable plot, or clean out his pipe, or engage in any of those other pleasant pursuits which those who do not write see as being equally important as, and considerably more difficult than, the production of readable writing. And when these cheery amateurs do put pen to paper, the result all too often reflects this happy-go-lucky approach. So the prospect of reading thirty-one juvenile attempts filled me with a nameless dread. I would leave them until later, I told myself, when I had leisure to do them justice, and perhaps when a glass of something both soothing and stimulating had done its work; a large measure of Teacher's, perhaps, would not be entirely inappropriate. Good Lord! I told myself, only a day in the profession and I was making schoolmaster's puns already. I must guard against that.

All this ran through my head in much less time than it takes to write, or read, about it all. I fancy that I had smiled to myself at my thoughts, for I noticed the boys exchanging amused glances, and I realized that I was now centre stage, as it were, and that any little mannerisms would soon be picked up and caricatured.

I squared my shoulders, metaphorically speaking, and assumed as stern an expression as I could manage. Dr Longton had given me a note of what the boys had studied, and what they were to study; and moreover I had consulted some of my friends and acquaintances who were, or had been, teachers, so that I had a memorandum of how I ought to proceed. Under cover of my desk, I now consulted this crib.

'Ah, yes,' I told my class. 'The study of English, as you

know, may be arbitrarily divided into language and literature. I see that your set books for this year are –' another glance at my notes here – 'yes.' The first on my list was *Pride and Prejudice* by Jane Austen, and a copy of the work itself lay conveniently to hand; a slim volume, and a small one, so that should present no great difficulty. Apart from one. 'I confess, boys,' I told them, 'that it is many years since I looked into this excellent work.' This was not literally true. I had never read the damned thing, nor indeed felt the least inclination to do so. 'If, therefore, you could read your grammar books for a moment or two, to permit me to refresh my memory?'

There was a groan at this, but they obeyed, reluctantly. I turned a page, and read. Back to the start, and read again. I turned the page over. I had slept badly, as I have told you, and I seemed to have some difficulty focusing on the small print. I shook my head to pull myself together, and closed the book. 'Very worthy, of course,' I said, 'but perhaps we might leave it for later in the term. What else have we on the reading list? Ah, Longfellow's *Hiawatha*, I see. Right: "By the shores of –" Glitchy Gloomy? Gitchy – h'mm. "By the –", yes! Perhaps not. Now, this is more like it. *Henry IV*, to be sure. A stirring tale, you will agree?'

The faces in front of me did not seem entirely sympathetic to this point of view. I had had enough of this. 'Well,' I demanded, 'what's wrong with that one?'

One of the boys, bolder than the rest, ventured, 'The language is a bit quaint, is it not, sir?'

'Ah, well, I grant you that. But it is several hundred years old, you know.'

'Do you think they really spoke like that, sir?' asked another.

I considered this. 'I don't imagine they did, now you come

to mention it. I suspect that it was partly a desire to produce Literature with a capital "L", and partly that Shakespeare felt that his characters were so much larger than life that they should behave, and speak, a little out of the ordinary. But it's a marvellous story, you know, when once you get beyond the quaintness of the dialogue. Here's a man, an important man too, a king in the play, but he might equally well be a millionaire businessman or something. He wants his lad to follow his father's footsteps, take over the business, as it were, when the father dies, or grows old, but the son won't have any of it. Instead, he runs wild, takes up with an elderly rakehell – wastrel, I mean – and then, when the father runs into trouble, and everyone thinks the son will let him down yet again, he comes back with a vengeance and discards his old friends.'

I looked round. They seemed a touch more inclined to be sympathetic now, but perhaps still not entirely convinced. I sighed. 'Very well, part of my task is to develop your youthful critical faculties. What sort of books and stories do you like?' I nodded to the nearest boy.

'Well, sir.' He hesitated, then with a sudden eagerness, 'I like the stories in the *Strand* magazine, sir.'

'The *Strand*, eh? What about the rest of you?'

There seemed general agreement on this point. 'And why is that, do you think?' I persisted.

That puzzled them for a moment, then, 'Easy to read,' said one, and 'No long words,' and 'Exciting tales,' came from various parts of the room.

'There you are,' said I. 'They are easy to read because their writers understood the rules of grammar, which you will be learning soon. As for the plots, the tales themselves, many of the themes echo the classic subjects which you will meet in Shakespeare and the other great writers. Which stories d'you like best?' I added, curious on this point.

'Sherlock Holmes!' came a dozen voices.

'Why, most of those are ten years old,' I told them. 'Well enough written of course, or at any rate the critics have been kind enough to think so. As for plots, Holmes's life has been sufficiently exciting to need no – or at any rate, very little – embellishment.'

'Do you know Mr Holmes, then, sir?' someone asked.

A great stillness seemed to descend on the room. I cursed myself bitterly for the fool that I was. I should have seen this coming, I told myself. I temporized, 'I have some nodding acquaintance with Dr Watson.'

They gazed at me with something like awe. Flattering, of course. Very flattering; I cannot and do not deny that. But very dangerous ground, none the less. I added hastily, 'I should perhaps say that my acquaintance is of the sketchiest,' but that did not seem to lessen their amazement.

At that point, I was saved by the bell for the next class. The boys filed out, with many a sidelong glance at me. I could pretty well understand their attitude. Here was I, an unknown elderly teacher, no special attributes or qualities, and it turned out that I was a friend of their hero, one of the greatest men of all time! No wonder they were silent as they left the room.

But I had blundered, and badly, I knew that. I mopped my brow at the thought. I could only hope that my disclaimer had some effect and that the tale did not spread round the school and come to the notice of the staff.

Meantime, I had other classes to take. If I have set down my initial experience at some length here, that is partly because it set the pattern for the rest of the day. I had four more classes, boys of various ages, and I used the same approach with each class, asking them to tell me what books and stories they liked, and discussing the reasons for that enjoyment – although I made very sure that I did not mention the *Strand* again! If they thought me odd, then at least they thought me an odd teacher, and to my newly refurbished grammatical mind the noun seemed to me to be more important than the adjective. In a word, I bluffed my way through the day.

There is another reason for my setting these events down here, and that a more sinister one, for my innocent reference to Holmes had a consequence later, as you will see.

For all that I had taken four or five classes without any incident other than the one which I have just related, I was ready enough for my dinner, and a pipe of tobacco, and a drink, and above all just a blessed rest, when the final bell of the scholastic day sounded. I took my books and papers back to my rooms, intending to relax before dinner, but found that the fire had not been lit. I put a match to it, but it was a cold day, and I felt disinclined to wait until the room should have warmed up. I knew that there was a fire burning in the Senior Common Room, and so I piled some coals on my own fire, so that the room would be pleasantly warm and welcoming on my return, then took pipe and pouch, and, as an afterthought, a sheaf of those essays which I had collected from my pupils, and set off across the quadrangle.

I had not gone more than a dozen yards, when I spotted my old friend, the mysterious Mr Tromarty. It was about half past four by this time, and the quadrangle was quite dark, so that Tromarty, who was going in the same direction as I was, would be unlikely to see me even if he looked round. To make doubly sure, I found such cover as there was in the angles of the wall and so on. It seemed to me very much as if Tromarty were heading towards those ruins of which Graves had spoken earlier, and this suspicion grew stronger as Tromarty left the neighbourhood of the school buildings and headed across the playing field, now all brown and muddy. I had to follow him, but feared that, even with the aid of darkness, I should be seen out in the open. I therefore slowed my pace and allowed Tromarty to increase the distance between us. I had been right in my surmise, though, for it was towards the little spinney which contained the ruins that my quarry now headed.

I increased my speed, and made for a sort of rustic pavilion, a shed used by the groundsman or possibly the school cricket team, as I supposed. Arrived at this, I sheltered in its lee for a moment, and could just make out that Tromarty had indeed entered the spinney, thus confirming all my suspicions. I could not let him get away with it, whatever 'it' might be, and set off after him accordingly.

However, as I turned the corner of the shed, I bumped – quite literally – into two boys who were lurking in the shadows, just as I had been. I had met a good many boys that day, and had no hope of remembering all their various names, but I recognized these two at once, for they were none other than Watson Minor and Edmonds, from my own Third form. 'What on earth are you doing out here?' I asked in some surprise. 'Should you not be doing your prep?'

They shuffled their feet and gazed at the ground in silence. I nodded at Edmonds. 'Either your trousers are on fire, boy, or you failed to extinguish the cigar whose aroma is offending my nostrils.'

Edmonds started, but said nothing. 'Give it here,' I said, holding out my hand.

Edmonds reluctantly handed over what our American friends call a 'stogie', a short, squat, evil-smelling thing that insulted the name of 'cigar'. I took a cautious experimental puff at it. 'Good God! Where on earth did you buy this thing?'

'The shop in the village, sir,' said the unhappy Edmonds. 'Threepence for four.'

'You were robbed,' I assured him. He stared at me in silence. I considered. These boys were thirteen or fourteen, and I suppose my own first unhappy attempts at smoking were made at about that age. I could not stop them trying the weed, but I could at least try to influence their taste. I tapped my pockets, and found my case. 'Here,' and I handed them each a decent torpedo-shaped Cuaba. 'But don't tell anyone that I gave them to you.'

If they had been surprised at my finding them, they were astonished at my reaction. For my part, I wanted desperately to follow Tromarty, see what he might be up to, but I hesitated to do so in the presence of these lads.

'Beg pardon, sir,' said Watson Minor as I stood there undecided, 'but was it Mr Tromarty you were wanting?'

'Tromarty? No, no. Why do you ask that?'

'Mr Tromarty just went by, and I thought you might want to speak to him.' Watson Minor waved a hand. 'He's on his way back to the school, sir, in any event.'

I looked where he pointed, and in the dim light I could see the tall, spare figure of Tromarty scuttling back towards the school buildings. 'No, no,' I repeated, 'I wasn't follow – I mean, I had not wished to speak to Mr Tromarty. Just getting a little air, that's all. Still, he has the right idea, for it is a trifle chilly outside. I think I'll go back as well. Don't stay out here too long, will you?' And I returned to my room, which was now at a reasonable temperature, and lit my pipe.

FIVE

If I had been elated at the thought that my deductions regarding Tromarty had been proved correct, I was now somewhat mystified that he had hastened away from the old abbey ruins with such precipitation. I relit my pipe, which had gone out as I puzzled over this unexpected speediness. It seemed to me that there were two logical explanations. Either Tromarty had seen me following, and cut short whatever nefarious activity he had in mind; or his business in the little spinney had been quickly concluded. I was rather inclined to dismiss the first possibility, for I flattered myself that I had been careful, but then Tromarty may possibly have heard my talk with the two boys, although I should not have credited him with such very acute hearing. The second possibility was more like it; if he had arranged a meeting, let us say, with some confederate, then it need not last very long, only long enough to give some instructions or hand over a note or message. That was not so very unlikely. Tromarty would not want to attract attention to himself by being seen going into the spinney and remaining there for a long time, but a fleeting visit, something which might seem merely an absent-minded wandering into the little wood during a constitutional, would be easily enough explained to any enquirer. A knock at the door interrupted my musings. I opened the door, to see Miss

Windlass standing there. 'Ah,' said I, intelligently enough. I glanced back into my study, unsure as to the propriety of asking her to step inside, but not wanting to leave her standing there in the corridor.

'I shall not keep you, sir,' she told me. 'It is a matter which concerns a couple of the boys in your charge, Watson Minor and Edmonds.'

'Indeed?' Scarcely better, but I did not know what else to say.

'Indeed,' said Miss Windlass severely. 'They both reported sick this evening, and will miss dinner.'

'Did they, and will they, by Jove?' Feeling that I was not doing very well at all here, and that more was required of me, I added, 'Anything serious?'

'I should judge not, Mr Harris. It strikes me that their symptoms are perfectly consistent with their having experimented with strong tobacco. From the odour which clings about their persons, I should judge it to have been cigars which wrought the mischief.'

'Ah. I see,' I managed. 'Well, growing boys, you know. Boys will be boys.'

'Under ordinary circumstances, I should have reported this to the head, for I regard it as a very serious business. However, since it is your first day at the Abbey School, I thought you might care to handle the matter yourself. Of course, should you wish me to do so, I shall inform the head at once.'

'Good Lord, no! That is to say, I should really prefer to handle this myself. They'll know about it, I promise you.'

'I thought you might see things in that light, sir.'

'Very good of you,' I mumbled. 'Save my bacon, so to speak? Yes, very good of you. You may be sure that I'll deal with them appropriately.'

'They are still in the sanitarium,' Miss Windlass told me. 'Both boys have been rather ill.'

'I see.' On surer ground now, I told her, 'Senna and castor oil, that's what they need. Finest thing out.'

Miss Windlass's face, which was by no means unattractive, positively lit up. 'My own prescription exactly!' she told me. And then, 'Have you some medical skill yourself, sir?'

I had rent my cloak of secrecy quite enough that day. I told her, 'In India one had to have some skill in that direction, although I can claim no sort of qualification. A strong draught is very often efficacious, in my limited experience.'

'I have already dosed them suitably,' said Miss Windlass, almost affably.

Emboldened by her amiability, I asked her, 'Do you normally report cases of sickness to the headmaster? I ask lest anything of the sort arises in future.'

'Oh, yes. Dr Longton is always kept informed of illnesses. In this instance, of course, where the matter is somewhat different, I use my own discretion.'

'Well, I am very glad that you came to me,' I said, quite truthfully. Miss Windlass smiled, and turned as if to go. I asked, 'Miss Windlass, I have heard some curious tales concerning my predecessor, Mr Greville, was it? I wondered if you had observed any signs of odd behaviour in him, or anything of that sort?'

Miss Windlass stared at me, frowning.

I went on hastily, 'I do not ask out of idle curiosity, but rather because the circumstances seem to have been so very curious, and you yourself, with your medical skills and powers of observation, might well have spotted some telltale signs.'

Obvious flattery is seldom seen as such even by men, and never by women, and Miss Windlass seemed to soften at this. 'No,' she told me, 'I cannot say that I ever observed anything out of the ordinary about the unfortunate young man. Had I done so, I should of course have informed Dr Longton.'

'Yes, I suppose so. So you have no sort of explanation at all, then?'

Miss Windlass shook her head. 'Rumour has it that Mr Greville was a secret drinker, but I attach little validity to that. However, it would explain much.' And she shook her head again, sadly, and bade me farewell.

I sat down, and resumed my earlier speculations. I had arrived at the conclusion that Tromarty had met some confederate in the little spinney, and it seemed to me that would make perfect sense if Tromarty were to have an accomplice. However reprobate the man himself might be, he was none the less elderly and rather puny, not a man who could easily overpower a young, vigorous fellow such as I imagined the murdered man Greville must have been. Moreover, this accomplice must be what I think the City gents call 'an outside man', for if he were on the school staff then there would be no need for this clandestine creeping, it would be easy enough to arrange a private meeting indoors. Well, I thought, I had my inside man, Tromarty, so the next thing was to follow him – properly, next time – and identify his accomplice, get a description of the other man at the very least, a name and address if possible. The latter would entail following the second man, of course, for although Tromarty might use his associate's name in the course of conversation, I could hardly expect him to reveal the exact address in a casual meeting! Still, I thought I had done pretty well thus far, and the identification of Tromarty's henchman should present me with little real difficulty.

In that spirit of modest pride and determination to do even better, I set off for dinner. As I ate, I was conscious that one or two of my fellow diners were casting occasional glances in my direction. At first I thought nothing much of it, but then I glanced up to see Herr Wieland actually staring at me. He coughed, and his fair complexion flushed like any schoolgirl's. 'Your pardon, Herr Harris,' said he. 'I meant no offence, sir, but there is some story going round that you are a friend of the renowned Sherlock Holmes.' And a great silence seemed to descend on the hall.

So that was it! Inwardly cursing myself, I managed a silly grin, and mumbled, 'I have a slight, a very slight, acquaintance with Dr Watson, sir. Nothing more exciting than that, I do assure you.'

Herr Wieland nodded, and smiled, and the room returned to normal. But I felt as if my carefully prepared disguise had been completely stripped away, leaving me exposed to the harsh glare of reality. I glanced down the table towards Tromarty, and saw him staring at me through his gold-rimmed spectacles. Damnation, I thought, he knows!

As I say, things returned to normal, probably very quickly at that, although to me the silence had seemed to last for an age. Herr Wieland began talking again about Germany and her colonial ambitions, although I cannot quite recall what started him off on that topic. He was quite determined that Germany should have her colonies and her empire, and had I not already identified Tromarty as my man, I think that my suspicions about Herr Wieland may well have been stirred. That apart, the rest of the meal passed without anything remarkable occurring, and I heaved a sigh of relief as we filed out, thankful that the prospective danger seemed to have passed off without any real harm being done.

Rather than risk further embarrassing questions about Holmes in the Senior Common Room, I returned to my own study. I had scarcely lit my pipe when there was a tap at my door. Wondering who this might be, and resolved to be on my guard, I opened the door, and was surprised to see Watson Minor and Edmonds standing there, both clutching their stomachs, and both looking very pale and wan.

'Come in,' I said, and when they were inside and I had closed the door, I added, 'I won't ask if you'll smoke, boys. I trust this has taught you a lesson?' I waved them to chairs.

'It's taught me one, sir,' said Edmonds frankly. 'I'll never touch the deuced stuff again.' He flushed. 'Sorry, sir, I mean I'll never touch the stuff again.'

'Ah, you say that now,' I told him, 'but you may think differently when you're older, my boy.' I became aware that I was waving my pipe for emphasis, and jammed it into my jacket pocket. 'Well, no permanent harm seems to have been done, indeed some good may have come of this if indeed it has put you off trying the weed again. So –' and I started to get to my feet.

Watson Minor said, 'Please, sir, we came to say "thank you" for not reporting us to the head.'

And Edmonds nodded vigorously in agreement.

I sat down again. 'As to that,' I began, 'I –' and then I realized that they were unaware that my own position might have been a trifle awkward. There was no point confusing them with details, I thought, so they might just as well continue to think that I had done them a kindness. It might well make it easier to ask them questions later on, after all. I cleared my throat noisily, and went on, 'Think nothing of it, boys.'

'It could have been a bit tricky,' said Edmonds, 'with Miss Windlass, and the head, and so on.'

'Well, if you ask me, the best thing is to forget the whole business. Just so long as you're both feeling better now. Yes?' They nodded. It occurred to me that this was probably as good a time as any to start asking some questions, while they were both feeling grateful towards the teacher who had not given them away. Quite deceitful of course, but then Holmes himself has often done similar things! 'Tell me,' I went on, 'you must have known young Whitechurch quite well?'

They exchanged glances, but did not reply.

'You see, I have heard some very curious tales,' I continued, 'which did not seem to me to ring quite true. I should be very grateful if you could enlighten me as to the real explanation.'

'Well,' said Watson Minor hesitantly, 'I never thought that old Whitechurch was a thief, sir.'

'He wasn't!' said Edmonds stoutly. 'The whole thing was what Papa calls a ramp. Whitechurch was made to look guilty.'

'Oh? And by whom?' I asked.

Edmonds shrugged his shoulders. 'Don't know, sir.'

'My brother, Watson Major, I mean, thought it was curious too,' said Watson Minor.

'And he said –' Edmonds broke off, glancing at his friend as if he had said too much.

'Look here,' I told them, 'if there is something odd about this Whitechurch business, it might be as well to thrash it out, just like those chaps in the *Strand* that we were talking about in class. Wouldn't it be a fine thing to solve the mystery?'

Edmonds grinned at this, but said, 'Trouble is, sir, I don't know any more about it. All I know is that it wasn't him. Whitechurch, I mean.'

'But there are other odd things happening here, sir,' ventured Watson Minor.

'Are there, indeed? What sort of odd things?'

Watson Minor seemed reluctant to continue.

I told him, 'You might just as well tell me whatever it was you were going to tell me. I give you my word that it will go no further, unless of course it is something very serious.'

'Well, sir, Bertie, my brother, I mean, was saying that there are some curious things happening, but he wouldn't tell us just what he meant.' Watson Minor stopped.

'Is that all?' I was frankly disappointed. 'Tell me, have you ever heard any sort of stories about the old abbey ruins at all? Anything of that sort?'

'Oh, some of the younger boys tell tales, of course,' said Edmonds.

'Yes,' I said, 'I thought it looked the sort of place that might have an odd reputation, might be thought to be haunted, or that kind of thing.'

'We don't believe in ghosts, sir,' said Edmonds with a certain amount of contempt.

'No, no, of course not. Silly stories. But some of the younger boys do think there's something along those lines, you say? Ghosts, or something?'

Watson Minor answered this. 'Not ghosts, sir, no. But they tell odd stories about the ruins, the old monks and so on.'

'You don't believe them?'

'No, sir!' He hesitated, then added, 'But I think there's some sort of secret society at the school, sir.'

Edmonds dug him in the ribs at this.

I said, 'What sort of secret society?'

'Don't know, sir.'

Edmonds added, 'It's a secret, you see, sir.'

'I see. And neither of you are in on the secret? Not members of this mysterious society?'

'No, sir.'

'But there's some connection between the secret society and the ruins?'

'Don't know, sir.' It was evident from Edmonds's tone that I should hear no more from them at the moment.

'Well,' I said, starting to get up, 'if that's all, it doesn't seem so very odd to me.'

Watson Minor stared unhappily at me, making no attempt to rise from his chair.

'Something more, though?' I asked.

Watson Minor shuffled uneasily. He said, 'Sir, we – we saw Mr Greville the night he died.' It came out all at once, and I sat down hard.

'When was this? What time of day?'

Watson Minor gave a shrug, but Edmonds said, 'Around midnight, sir.'

'Good Lord! I understood that nobody had seen the poor fellow that night? And how came you to see him? It was long after lights out, was it not?'

'Yes, sir,' agreed Edmonds miserably.

'Having said this much, you had better tell me the rest, I think. I promise to let it go no further, but you must appreciate that I cannot repeat that promise in view of what you have just said. This is a serious matter, and you would be well advised to hold nothing back.'

'No, sir.' Edmonds still looked unhappy, but he went on, 'The thing is, sir, we were talking with Watson Major that morning, the morning of the day that Mr Greville died, I mean, and he – Watson Major – said there was something odd going on –'

'Devilish odd, he said, sir,' added Watson Minor helpfully.

Edmonds shot him a glance that silenced him. 'Anyway, we said that Mr Greville had said pretty much the same thing, and Watson Major seemed very interested to hear that, and told us not to talk about it with anyone else. Then, later on, Watson Minor here overheard Mr Greville muttering to himself, as he did sometimes, saying something like, "Tonight's the night", was it?' He appealed to Watson Minor, who nodded agreement.

'I did hear him, sir,' Watson Minor added, to me. '"Tonight's the night", just in those very words. And so we decided, Edmonds and me – I – to go out and see what was happening.'

'And we did,' Edmonds finished.

'You did go out? And you did see Mr Greville? Where was that?'

'In the quad, sir,' said Edmonds.

'Around midnight?'

'Yes, sir, about then.'

'Was he alone? How did he look?'

Edmonds glanced at Watson Minor, who nodded. 'He seemed to be waiting for someone, sir,' said Edmonds.

'And he was just standing there, waiting, was he?'

'Yes, sir.'

'Did he look – ill, or anything?' I asked, mindful of the fact that the dead man had supposedly smelled of whisky.

'No, sir,' said Edmonds. 'He just looked at his watch every so often.'

'Tell me,' I asked cautiously, 'have you ever seen a man who's had a drop too much to drink?'

'Oh, yes, sir!'

'You have?'

'My brother, sir,' said Watson Minor with a grin.

'And Papa, one Christmas,' added Edmonds. 'And the village blacksmith back home.'

'And the carter's man.'

'And the porter.'

'I see. That will do to be going on with, thank you. What I want to know is just this – did Mr Greville seem at all the worse for drink that night?'

'No, sir,' they answered in unison.

Edmonds added, 'That was one of the things we didn't believe, sir, when the story got out. He hadn't been drinking, sir.'

'Well, then, how is it that you said nothing?' I wanted to know.

They exchanged glances. 'It was a bit awkward, sir,' mumbled Watson Minor, 'What with Whitechurch just being sent down, and then us being out after lights out.'

'And it wasn't as if we could tell anyone anything important,' said Edmonds. 'All we saw was Mr Greville standing there, waiting, and then he went to the side door near his rooms, and met someone, and they went inside. If there had been anything else, we would have said, and faced the music, sir.'

'What? He met someone, you say?'

'Yes, sir, but we didn't see who it was,' said Edmonds.

'If we had done,' repeated Watson Minor, 'we would have said something, even if it meant getting into trouble. We would, sir!'

'Yes, I'm sure you would. You did the right thing, I'm sure. Tell me, could you see if it was an old man that Mr Greville met, or a young one?'

'A young one, sir.' The answer came immediately from Edmonds.

'Watson?'

'Yes, sir, it was a young man. I thought perhaps Mr Wieland, or Mr Carstairs. But I couldn't see just who it was.'

'Or Mr Reed?' I suggested.

'It couldn't be Mr Reed, sir,' Watson Minor pointed out, 'because he lives in the village, and goes home each evening.'

'Ah yes, of course. You didn't notice if his hair was dark or fair, say?'

'It was too dark, sir,' said Watson Minor. 'The moon was shining, but that side of the building was in the shadows.'

'But you're certain he was a young man?'

'Yes, sir.'

'Thin? Stout? Tall or short?'

'Just – sort of ordinary, sir,' said Watson Minor, frowning.

'H'mm.'

'And, sir,' added Edmonds, with some reluctance, 'I think I heard the noise that Mr Greville made when he – you know, sir.'

'Good Lord, really?'

'I'm not sure, sir. But when we got back to our room, I couldn't get to sleep, and I heard a kind of noise.'

'What kind of noise?'

'A thud, sir.'

'You didn't see the time, I suppose?'

'Yes, sir. I struck a match and looked at my watch. It was ten past one.'

'About an hour after you had seen Mr Greville?'

'Yes, sir.'

'I see. Well, boys, I think that is all. You did well to come to me with this information, as I said, but I would not mention it to anyone else, if I were you. We'll keep it between the three of us for the time being, shall we?'

They both seemed relieved at this, and took their leave. I sat down without bothering to light my pipe again, thinking over what they had said. If the two boys had seen Greville alive at midnight, and not under the influence, that rather tended to show that there had been mischief. Both boys seemed reliable enough witnesses, and I was inclined to accept their testimony that Greville was sober.

And then what of the mysterious man whom Greville had met? If he were young, and again I saw no reason to doubt the boys on that score, then it narrowed it down pretty much to Wieland, Carstairs or Reed, for the other members of staff could only charitably be described as 'middle-aged'. I could not dismiss Reed, for all that he slept at home in the village, for he could easily have returned. On the other hand, his presence would have been remarked upon.

That led me to Tromarty. How did he fit in? His figure was distinctive, the boys would know if the man whom Greville had met had been Tromarty. And if Tromarty were meeting Greville, how did that affect the significance of Tromarty's visit to the spinney? I could understand Tromarty's meeting Reed, who left the school premises at evening, in the spinney when the day was over – no, I couldn't! If Tromarty wanted to speak to Reed, he could have done it quite well during the day.

But then, why could Greville also not meet whoever it

was during the day, instead of creeping about the quadrangle at midnight? And that just before Christmas, the darkest and murkiest time of the year? I decided to leave Tromarty and the spinney for the moment, and concentrate on Greville. If Greville had merely wanted to speak to a colleague, why did he not do so at a civilized hour, and in congenial surroundings? Answer, because there was more to it than a mere conversation; Greville suspected mischief that very night, and had determined to investigate. The second man? A confederate, a partner in the investigation? Or a villain, who had lured Greville from his bed with some tale, in order to make away with him? On the face of it, the latter seemed more likely, for if it were a friend whom Greville had met, why should that friend not come forward, speak as to having seen Greville that night? But again, if the villainy were still continuing, such a putative friend might still be actively pursuing the enquiry.

One thing was certain, and that was that my next task was to interview Wieland, Reed and Carstairs, ask if they had seen Greville on the night he died. Not that I expected any of them to tell me so! Friend or enemy, if they had not spoken to the head or to Holmes, they would scarcely blurt it out to plain Mr Harris. No, but I could observe them for signs of guilt, or surprise, for some response to my unexpected questions.

I stood up. Herr Wieland had the rooms directly opposite mine, and I saw by my watch that the evening was still young. I went out into the corridor, and tapped on Wieland's door.

SIX

'*Herein, bitte!*'

I opened the door, and looked round it.

'Oh, please, Herr Harris, come in! Sorry to greet you in German, but I use it with the boys as much as possible. It is the only way to teach a language.'

'Oh, of course, of course.'

'Please, sit down.' Wieland waved me to a chair. 'Whisky? A cigar? I did not see you in the Senior Common Room this evening,' he added.

'No. Truth to tell, I was a touch embarrassed by the attention I received at dinner. I'm not very remarkable, you know, it's just that some of my friends have a certain reputation.'

'I understand perfectly.' Wieland hesitated. 'I myself sometimes avoid the others, I am a bit of an outsider, a foreigner. And my views are well known.'

'But in general you get on with them?'

'Get on? Oh, yes, I get on with everyone.'

'Were you a particular friend of Greville, the poor chap whom I replaced?' I asked casually.

Wieland frowned. 'I could not say we were special friends. We "got on", as you put it. We both had an interest in golf, though neither of us had any great skill, I fear, and that brought us together at times. But apart from that, no.'

'So you did not meet him on the night he died?'

'No!' Wieland's surprise was evident. 'Who told you that I did?'

'Oh, nobody. I just wondered, that was all. Someone said that they thought he might have met someone, you know.'

Wieland's frown deepened. 'Who said this?'

'I couldn't tell you. Just something I heard in passing really, that was all. Probably nothing.'

'I am sure that if anyone had met Greville that night, they would have said something, to Dr Longton, or at the inquest. Would they not?'

'I'm sure you're right,' I agreed. 'Thank you for the drink, and the cigar. Pop into my rooms some time, and I'll return the compliment.' And with that, I took my leave.

I went back to my own rooms. I felt sure that Herr Wieland had told me the truth, that he had not seen Greville on the night the latter died. A pity, in some ways, I thought, for Wieland would have been an ideal candidate. Not that I am anti-German, or anti-anything for the matter of that, but if there were something underhand going on, then if a man who was not English, and whose country had some animosity towards England, were involved, at least I could have seen some logic in it!

Reed, I knew, had left hours ago for his home in the village. However, Carstairs should still be up and about, it lacked five or ten minutes to 'lights out' for the boys as yet. I made my way to Carstairs's rooms, then, and tapped upon his door. 'Come in!'

I went in, and Carstairs, a pipe in his mouth, a newspaper in his hand, and a look of slight surprise upon his face, rose from his chair. 'Anything wrong?'

'Good Lord, no,' I told him. 'Just passing the time of day, as it were.'

'Well, then, take a pew.' Carstairs threw the newspaper into a corner. 'Whisky? Cigar?'

'I've just finished a cigar, thanks, but a whisky would be very pleasant.'

Carstairs busied himself with decanter and gasogene. 'How are you settling in?'

'Oh, not half as bad as I feared.'

He laughed. 'Of course, your telling the boys that you knew Mr Sherlock Holmes cannot have done your stock any harm.'

I almost spilled my whisky. 'I thought I had made it clear that I am only slightly acquainted with Dr Watson?' I said carefully.

'I'm sure you're just being modest. Do you not know Holmes at all?' He looked at me over the match he was applying to his pipe.

'Well – I mean, I've met him.' I squared my shoulders, metaphorically if not literally. 'Look here, Carstairs, it has come to my attention that you may have met young Greville the night he died.'

Carstairs's reaction was very different from that of Wieland earlier. He did not speak for a moment, and then, an odd note in his voice, he asked me, 'May I ask just how it came to your attention, Mr Harris?'

'I'm afraid I cannot answer that,' I said stiffly. 'My association with Holmes – and Watson, too, of course – has made me something of a busybody, I fear, and I seem to accumulate these little bits of information. Did you see Greville that night?'

Carstairs lit another match, and took his time to get his pipe going to his satisfaction. 'I'm damned if I know how *you* know,' he said, 'but I did, as a matter of fact.'

'Around midnight?'

'About that time.' Carstairs leaned forward, and spoke earnestly. 'Look here, Mr Harris, I didn't say anything at the time, or later at the inquest, because I was scared. Greville had come to see me earlier that day. He seemed in a very edgy, nervous state, talking all sorts of nonsense –'

'What sort of nonsense?'

'Oh, I don't know. Said people were "after him", that sort of thing. I'd have said he'd been drinking.'

'Did he drink?'

'No, I can't say that he did. But his behaviour, you know, was so very odd that I couldn't explain it any other way. Now, of course, with hindsight, I can see that he was most probably ill, brain fever or something of that sort. Why else would he jump from the tower like that? To think that I might have saved him! I blame myself, you know. That's partly why I kept quiet about seeing him.'

'Ah, yes, you were telling me about that.'

'Yes. He insisted that I meet him that night, to "investigate fully", as he put it.'

'Why you?' I asked. 'Why did he not go to the headmaster, tell him what he suspected?'

'There you have me. Possibly with my being more his own age, he felt happier? I couldn't say. Anyway, I tried to talk him out of it, to tell him there was nothing to worry about, but he insisted, as I say, became quite upset until I agreed, just to shut him up. Well, I met him as he said, around midnight, at a side door – all very cloak and dagger, but he insisted – and I brought him here. I gave him a glass of whisky, and tried again to calm him down.'

'Ah, so it was you who gave him the whisky?'

'Yes, to try to settle his nerves. But it was only a very

small one, not half of what you've got there. Not enough to make a mosquito tipsy! Anyway, it seemed to work, he settled down a bit, and then he said he was going to bed.'

'And that was all?'

'That was all I had to do with it. He left me here, and I thought about it a moment or so, decided it was a shame, a good man going to the dogs like that, then I went off to my own bed.'

'You didn't think to accompany Greville back to his rooms?'

'It simply never occurred to me,' said Carstairs frankly. 'As I say, he seemed to have settled down a lot, and his rooms are just down the corridor. Why should I suspect that he would – do what he did?'

'You are convinced that he killed himself, then?'

'Absolutely. What other explanation could there possibly be?'

'You dismiss the notion that someone did intend him some harm?'

'Oh, come on, Mr Harris!' Carstairs laughed, then grew serious again. 'I am sorry, it is no laughing matter, I know. But you cannot honestly imagine that anyone at the Abbey School had anything to do with poor Greville's tragic death? Apart from him, I mean.'

'It is a curious coincidence, though, is it not? Greville tells you that he feels himself threatened, and then he dies in that very strange fashion?'

'So you unhesitatingly conclude that this mysterious "someone" killed him?' Carstairs did not bother to hide his contempt. He leaned forward. 'Look here, Mr Harris, I kept quiet about the whole thing just because it would have confirmed what everyone suspected, the coroner included, though he tried to spare the feelings of Greville's family. The man was unhinged. He came to me for help, and I more or less sent him off with a flea in his ear. It reflects badly upon me, I agree, but that was not the reason for my silence. Had I spoken, it would have been glaringly obvious that the man committed suicide whilst the balance of his mind was disturbed, as I believe the correct phrase goes. When I think about it, I'm rather sorry that I gave him that whisky. He was no drinker, and it may just have been that small glass which tipped the scale, caused him to take that fatal decision. I'm not proud of that, Mr Harris, and I don't propose to advertise the fact that I had anything to do with it. Nor do I intend to do anything that might change the "accidental death" verdict. Now, I've laid the facts before you, and if you want to make them public, there's nothing I can do to stop you.'

I thought about it for a moment. Carstairs's testimony had the ring of truth. There was no point causing Greville's relatives more distress, not without more evidence one way or another. 'I'll say nothing for the time being,' I told Carstairs, 'although I should have been inclined to tell the truth at the outset, were I in your shoes. Now, we can put Greville here at midnight, or soon after. Some time later that night, he fell from the tower. So he must have left his own rooms, if indeed he ever returned to them.'

'That much is certain. As I say, I never thought to walk back to his rooms with him, so I cannot say one way or the other.'

'H'mm.' There seemed little point pursuing the matter, and so I said 'good night', and went back to my rooms. I did not go immediately to bed, though, as you may readily imagine. Instead I sat gazing at the dying embers of the fire, and tried to put my thoughts into some sort of order.

If nothing else, I had at least discovered the identity of the man Greville had met that fateful night. More, for up until now, nobody, apart from the two rather frightened boys, had even known that Greville had met anyone.

The next task was to consider Carstairs's statement, and his bearing. He had been hesitant at first, but that was only to be expected; but then he had answered me readily enough. As a working hypothesis only, then, I took Carstairs's statement at its face value; Greville had been in a nervous frame of mind. Possibly more than that, he may have been suffering from – what was it my alienist colleagues labelled it – paranoia? The delusion that one is being watched, followed, persecuted. I could accept that, for I've seen some odd things in my time.

Next, Carstairs had given Greville, who was unused to spirits, some whisky to calm him down. Now, I privately thought it very likely that Carstairs may actually have given Greville considerably more than he had indicated to me. The 'stiff drink to settle one's nerves' is well enough known; but the embarrassed Carstairs would naturally wish to minimize his own contribution to Greville's condition, and had thus pretended to me that it was a small measure he had served to Greville. Assume that the whisky had *not* settled Greville's nerves, that it had the opposite effect and made him yet more jumpy. We have all experienced that, I fancy? Very well, Greville returned to his rooms, but was unable to settle down to sleep. His old phantasms, whatever ghosts and ghouls that he imagined were haunting him, came again as he sat there alone. In desperation, he fled from them. It was useless to ask his colleagues for help, he had already asked Carstairs, and been told, in effect, to pull himself together. He very likely had some notion of escaping by climbing the tower, and when he reached the top, found he had nowhere to go, except –

I shuddered. It was not so very ridiculous, though. Or perhaps he really had slipped; it may, as the coroner had said, have been a genuine accident.

Either way, it made sense, a good deal more sense than all this talk of murder and conspiracy and Lord alone knew what else. I reviewed the other odd aspects, trying to clear up loose ends. The gossip about 'something going on', for example? Easy enough to explain: you get that sort of thing in the army, in hospitals, in any large business concern; it is human nature to grumble about one's superiors, one's colleagues, when all is said and done. Tromarty? A harmless old man! Why, I myself had scoffed at my own foolish fancies when they first obtruded upon my mind. The name was, just as I had told myself, a coincidence. And his visit to the spinney? Well, it was no true 'visit', as I have told you; he merely went in and came out again. Most likely he had been taking a constitutional after being cooped up indoors all day; nothing so very strange about that, was there? And the matter of young Lord Whitechurch and the alleged theft of money? That probably had nothing whatever to do with Greville's sad death. I did not know the rights and wrongs of the Whitechurch business, it is true, but then neither did Holmes; it had puzzled him too, so I need not feel too bad about that.

However, I was fairly certain that I had solved the more important riddle, that of Greville's death. I stood up, pretty well satisfied with myself. Tomorrow, I would telegraph to Holmes, tell him that his clients were mistaken, and the death had indeed been a tragic accident. Or suicide? Well, there was surely no need whatever to cause further distress to the young man's family. And the circumstances meant that a better man than I would be sorely puzzled to know the exact truth. No, 'accidental death' had been the coroner's verdict, and it might just as well be mine.

As I say, I was well pleased with myself. But something nagged at me, and as I prepared for bed, I remembered what it was. Watson Minor had mentioned an elder brother, said that this brother had also had some misgivings, and had been very interested to learn that Greville was uneasy. I would do the thing properly. I would speak to this Watson Major tomorrow, and clear up the last little particle of doubt. That settled, I slept like the proverbial log, until my alarm woke me next day.

I could not tell you just how I managed my teaching duties that second day. The first day of the new term, and my first acquaintance with the boys in my charge, had been made easy by the novelty of it all. A little informality, a little scrappiness, even, could be expected and excused. But now things were somewhat more settled, and everyone – myself excepted, perhaps – anticipated that we should evolve our own routine of class work, fall into our appointed roles as teacher and pupils. It was all right for the boys, of course, they knew well enough what was expected of them! But I, to be frank, had not the slightest clue as to how to proceed. You see, I had fully expected that the investigation would take up the bulk of my time, and that the teaching would, as it were, be merely secondary. I now realized that such was not the case.

However, by avoiding the grammar and syntax side of things as much as possible, and concentrating instead on the set books, I managed to get through the lessons some-how or other. The boys, I think, were not too displeased at my methods, for although I am no grammarian my recording of Holmes's cases has at least made me aware of what appeals to a youthful readership. I involved the boys in discussions of the merits and otherwise of the various works they had to read, and the hours passed pleasantly enough, so that I flattered myself that if I could but 'mug up' on the grammar – for I was unconsciously absorbing some of the boys' phrases and usages – I might make a pretty useful sort of English teacher, given time.

As I say, I got through the day without too many gaffes, and when the last lesson was over, I sought out Watson Minor, and asked if he would be so kind as to send his elder brother to my rooms.

Watson Minor exhibited some surprise at this request. 'I say, sir, there's nothing wrong, is there?' he asked anxiously. 'It wasn't about that other business, the thing with Edmonds and me, was it?'

'No, no,' I reassured him. 'Nothing of that kind. Just send him along, there's a good lad.'

Ten minutes later, Watson Major tapped upon my door, and I waved him to a chair. His face bore some indications of concern and surprise, I assumed because of the unexpected invitation, but he was a handsome enough young man of seventeen or eighteen, as I judged. Unless I was much mistaken, he had already turned a few of the village girls' heads, and in a year or so the Society ladies would be thinking seriously of his attributes as a prospective son-in-law.

'Sir?' he asked, as he entered the room. 'It's not about that young devil – I mean, my brother, is it?'

'No, nothing of that sort. Sit down, my boy, sit down.'

'Thank you, sir.'

'A cigar?' I asked, as he took a seat. 'Or would it spoil your appetite for dinner?'

His face showed real surprise at the offer. 'Very good of you, sir,' he stammered, 'but – well!'

'Oh, help yourself,' said I, throwing him my case. 'A decent cigar, now and then, does no real harm, not in my view. Just have to be careful not to overdo things, that's the secret.'

'Very kind,' he repeated, lighting the cigar in a way which indicated a certain degree of familiarity.

'Look here, Watson, I want to be frank with you. You have very likely heard some sort of talk about my being acquainted with Mr Sherlock Holmes and your namesake, Dr Watson? Well, I am here at Mr Holmes's express request.'

'I say!' Watson Major had evidently not expected this. He choked on his cigar, coughed, and sat back in his chair, trying to look nonchalant.

'It is a surprise, I know. But Mr Holmes has reasons for thinking that all is not as it should be at the Abbey School.'

Watson Major leaned forward. 'I don't know how he is involved, sir, or how he knows – although one might have expected that he *would* know, of course! But he, and you, are quite correct. There is something odd going on here.'

'Ahah! I thought you were the man I needed. What exactly is amiss, then?'

Watson Major shook his head. 'If I knew for certain, sir, I'd tell you like a shot,' he said. 'The trouble is, I don't know, not anything substantial, if that's the right word. Nothing I could put a name to, if you follow me, sir, just a sort of gnawing sense of unease.'

'Connected, perhaps, with the tragic death of Mr Greville?'

Watson Major started. 'That, yes, sir.'

'I understand that you and he shared these concerns that all was – is – not well?'

'It's very curious that you should say that, sir. On the day he died, Mr Greville had apparently let slip something in front of some of the boys, my brother, and Edmonds. Something about there being something odd, that kind of thing. Anyway, it coincided so exactly with what I'd been thinking that I determined to see Mr Greville that very day, try to thrash out what was wrong.'

'And did you? See him, I mean?'

Watson Major shook his head. 'I went to his rooms, and knocked, but there was no reply.'

'Wait – when was that?'

'Oh, after class. About this very hour, as a matter of fact. Half past four? About that. Anyway, there was no reply, and so I went on with my prep. I couldn't concentrate very much, I'm afraid, for thinking about things, You know how it is? Anyway, the more I thought about it, the sillier I felt! I shuddered at the thought that Mr Greville might have been in, might have answered my knock. For what would I have said to him? The trouble was, my thoughts were so – so nebulous, so unclear, just a sort of sensation of something wrong. In the event, of course, I think he'd have given me a sympathetic hearing, but I couldn't know that then. All I thought was, that I'd look foolish, telling a master these silly fancies. So I didn't try again.'

'You didn't return to Mr Greville's rooms that night?'

'No, sir. I felt so foolish, as I say, so I just tried to forget the whole thing. Afterwards, of course, I realized that something *had* been wrong, horribly wrong, for Mr Greville to die like that. But I didn't know just what. If it were suicide, and that seemed to be what everyone thought, even

though the coroner said it was an accident, then – I don't
know, I think I thought that if Mr Greville had been – you
know, wrong in the head, and killed himself in consequence, then perhaps my own fancies – well!'

'You feared that perhaps you, too, were going mad? That
it?'

Watson Major nodded, reluctant to speak.

'Well, I think we may dismiss that notion,' I told him.

'But I didn't, not then, you see, sir. I was thinking all
sorts of things. And then I didn't see that speaking out
would help. What could I say, that I thought something
was wrong, and Mr Greville agreed? That would just be
read as my seeing that Mr Greville was upset, suicidal.
That's what I thought. And then, with being afraid that I –
that I might be affected, as it were, myself – so I just kept
quiet, tried to forget the whole thing.'

'Pretend that nothing was wrong? Well, I can't blame
you for that. But tell me, what originally kindled your
suspicions, before Mr Greville died, I mean?'

'Sir?'

'Well, why did you first think that something, anything,
was wrong? What was the "something" which made you
uneasy?'

Watson Major frowned. 'It's hard to explain, sir. There
was that business with young Whitechurch, of course. Why
the devil should – sorry, sir – I mean why on earth should
he steal anything? His father's one of the richest men in all
England, and Whitechurch himself was never short of a
bob or two. It made no sort of sense. But that wasn't it, that
was merely the culmination, as you might say, of a whole
series of vague things.'

'What sort of things?' I persisted.

Watson Major shook his head. 'That's just it, sir, it's so hard to pin down. A sort of atmosphere, a feeling of secrecy; sneakiness, as the young 'uns would put it.'

'Ah. Ever heard of a secret society at the school?' I asked him.

'Who told you that?' He seemed shaken.

'Oh, just gossip one overhears, you know. Is there?'

'I think there is, now you mention it, sir.'

'Among the boys, of course?'

'I think so, sir. I'm not a member, of course, so I wouldn't know. You get these things, I expect, in most schools, but here nobody seems to know anything about it, if you follow me. Very secret, so to speak. But I've heard and seen odd things, snippets of conversation, fellows giggling like a bunch of sissies. Well, you get that sort of rotten thing at some schools, I suppose,' he added, in a tone that would not come amiss in a man of seventy, 'but I've never seen anything of that sort here, thank the Lord. So I suppose it must be a secret society of some sort, membership strictly by invitation only. And I'll tell you another thing, sir, I've an idea that young Whitechurch had been asked to join this mysterious society.'

'Ah! Why d'you say that?'

'He came to me, sir, a day or so before – before the trouble blew up. Introduced himself as a pal of my young brother, said he wanted a man-to-man chat with me. You know what these youngsters are like,' he added, with no trace of irony in his voice.

'Oh, indeed. Carry on.'

'Well, he asked, in a very roundabout sort of fashion, what did I think of clubs, societies, that sort of thing. I answered as best I could, said they were very fine in their way, but a fellow has to be careful to ensure that his sympathies agree with the club's objects, or there's likely to be a falling out.'

'Very sensible advice too.'

'Thank you, sir. Trouble was, he was so vague that I couldn't really make out what he was after, if you follow me, so I just gave him vague sort of advice in reply. Then a day or so later, there was all the fuss.'

'H'mm. Let me put this to you. Suppose that young Whitechurch had been approached to be a member of this secret society, and suppose that there was some sort of test, some initiation ceremony, involving some act of devilment, some daring exploit? Would that meet the case?'

'You mean he had to steal something in order to prove his worthiness for admission to the order?' Watson Major's face showed that he felt this unlikely.

'No?'

'I don't think so, sir,' he told me doubtfully. 'I suppose it could be so, but then there has never been anything of that sort at the school before, not in my time at any rate. And if theft, or something of the sort, were part of the admission procedure, then it should be a regular occurrence, shouldn't it, whenever a new candidate is proposed?'

'Yes, I suppose you're right there. Another point, though, and that concerns the ruins of the old abbey. Any stories about those?'

'Again, sir, it's funny you should mention those. There have always been tales about the old ruins, ever since I've known the place.'

'Linking them with this mysterious secret society?'

Watson Major shook his head. 'The secret society is not something the chaps talk about, sir,' he said. 'The ruins, though, they have an odd reputation. I suppose their being out of bounds would account for a lot of that.'

'Have you explored them?'

Watson Major looked at me.

'I shan't be angry if you have,' I told him. 'I'd just like to know, that's all.'

'I suppose most of the fellows have taken a peep at some time, sir. And I'm no exception, I must admit. Though not for years, of course,' he added hastily.

'But there is feeling that the ruins hold some secret?'

'Oh, yes, sir.'

'Well, Watson,' I said, getting to my feet, 'you've been candid with me, and I hope that you feel that I've been equally honest with you. I'll tell you what, though, let's just keep this conversation between the two of us, for the moment at any rate.'

'Right you are, sir!' Watson Major seemed relieved at this. He shook my proffered hand, glanced at the half of the cigar which remained, and ruefully deposited it in an ashtray. 'Best not walk the corridors with that, sir!'

'Indeed not. Well, mum's the word, my boy. You may have done more good this evening than you realize, but it will all be wasted if we blab about our little chat.'

'I'll remember, sir.'

I saw him to the door, and ushered him out. As I opened the door, I noticed a figure lurking – there is no other word for it – in the shadows at the other side of the corridor. I recognized the man at once. It was Tromarty. As I bade Watson Major farewell, Tromarty scuttled back out of sight.

I tried to show no surprise as I watched Watson Major go down the corridor. But as I closed the door and sat down again, I did some thinking. It had definitely been Tromarty out there, and he had definitely been watching my door. I could stake my life on that. *My* life? More to the purpose, if Tromarty were somehow involved in Greville's death, then young Watson Major might be at some risk, now he had been seen associating with me! It looked as if my latest theory that Greville's death had been accidental might need yet another hasty revision.

I got to my feet almost before I had sat down. One thing had emerged from Watson Major's account, and that was that the ruins had a curious reputation among the boys. I linked that reputation with the mysterious 'secret society', of whose existence I, and Holmes, had hitherto been unaware. And there might be yet another link to the mysterious Tromarty.

I might not be able to confront Tromarty just yet, I had no firm evidence, but I could do what I had earlier thought of doing and explore the ruins of the old abbey. It was nearly five o'clock, and now fully dark outside, so I should be able to do a little investigating unobserved.

I found a candle and matches, muffled myself up in coat, hat and scarf, picked up my stick, and let myself out by a side door. It was cold outside, with a hint of sleet in the air. I was, as you may imagine, in a somewhat excited frame of mind as I hurried across the quadrangle and round the side of the school buildings, and I had the distinct impression that someone was following me. I stopped, more than once, and tried to see who it might be, but beyond a general impression that someone was there, behind me, I could make nothing out.

I did not immediately dismiss the notion as mere fancy, though. I knew for a fact that Tromarty had been watching my rooms not twenty minutes earlier, and I strongly suspected that it was Tromarty who was dogging my footsteps now. I kept a careful eye open, you may be sure, as I made my way over the playing fields, now with a light dusting of white underfoot, and into the little spinney.

It was, of course, pitch black in there. Such light as there was in the sky came perhaps from the last rays of the sun reflecting from the rain clouds, perhaps from the moon's struggling to penetrate those clouds. In any event, there was a sort of ghastly grey tinge to the sky, which gave some fitful illumination out in the open fields, but which was completely useless once I was in amongst the trees. I was thus obliged to move at a snail's pace, groping my way almost from tree to tree. I had not the least idea where the ruins might be, but I knew that the little wood was so small that they could not be very far from the edge, and so it proved. After a dozen yards, I came into a sort of clearing, where the grey sky cast some sort of light, enabling me to see that here indeed were those ruins I sought. An unimpressive assemblage, resembling an untidy builder's yard. I struck a match to take a closer look, and as it flared up I distinctly heard a sound off to my left, as of someone treading on a twig or something of the sort.

'Who's there?' I called out, starting towards the sound and blowing the match out as I did so.

There was a second sound, similar to the first, a muffled footstep, but this time behind me, not in front. Two of them, then! Tromarty and the man I suspected him of meeting earlier, perhaps? This looked bad; there were two of them and only one of me, and I had no weapon but my stick. Useful enough as a stick, and as a makeshift defence, but I could have wished for my old revolver just then. I decided that discretion was better than valour, and made my way back to the ramshackle walls of the ruins, feeling a little safer when they were solidly behind me.

I strained my eyes in the darkness, trying to make out if

anyone was there. A muffled sound, a thud, off in the direction of the first sound? I could not be certain, but I fancied something of the sort. Then silence, a long silence.

After a time, and I assure you that it was a long time, I ventured towards where I had heard the first sound and the last. I was, as before, moving slowly from tree to tree, and looking round me in a very apprehensive fashion. I had gone perhaps twenty feet when I stumbled, literally, over some obstacle that lay upon the ground. I naturally put my hand out to save myself, and it encountered something unexpected. I have handled enough dead men in my army career to know a body when I touch one.

I scrambled up to a kneeling position, and struck a match. It was Tromarty, and he had been killed by a blow to the back of his head. 'Damnation!' was all I could manage by way of remark.

A sound in front of me brought me to my senses, and I blew the match out hastily.

'Who's there? I say, is anyone there?'

I recognized the voice. 'Watson Major? Is that you?'

'Yes, sir. Meade's with me.'

Meade, I knew, was a friend of Watson Major's, another strapping lad of seventeen or so. They could be relied upon, and I felt better for knowing that they were there. 'Don't come any closer,' I warned. 'There's been – been an accident.'

'Mr Harris? Is that you, sir?'

'More or less. Only my name isn't Harris. It's Dr John Watson, and I'm afraid we shall have to call the police – and Mr Sherlock Holmes – at once.'

SEVEN

'**W**ell, Watson –' began Mr Sherlock Holmes.

'Holmes,' I warned him, 'it has been a very long night, and I am feeling decidedly fragile. If you were about to make some remark about this being a "pretty kettle of fish", or something of that sort, I would strongly advise against it.'

I spoke no more than the literal truth. To begin with, I myself had, very naturally in the circumstances, come under some suspicion over Tromarty's death. The local police had been summoned, they had contacted Scotland Yard, and, at my request, Sherlock Holmes. In view of the social standing of the pupils at the Abbey School, the Yard had been only too glad to allow Holmes to take the case, had indeed dropped the case like the proverbial hot potato. Dr Longton, however, was by no means so eager to allow a private investigator into the school, and only the intervention of the Home Secretary, summoned by telephone from his bed in the very early hours of the morning, had managed to gain Holmes the headmaster's rather grudging co-operation. This had all happened in the course of the one crowded night, so you will see that I was a touch disquieted.

'On the other hand,' I added ruefully, 'if you were to mutter something about my making "a pretty hash" of things, I think that would be fully justified this time.'

'Come, Watson, you have not done at all badly.'

'Holmes, this poor, inoffensive old fellow is dead as a direct result of my incompetence!'

'Hardly that, Doctor.'

'Oh, yes, Holmes. Why, I suspected that he was Professor Moriarty come to life again, or one of his brothers – Moriarty's brothers, I mean – and all the time he was being hunted by the same man who killed Greville. I am to blame, Holmes, no doubt of that.'

He regarded me keenly. 'You never cease to surprise me, my dear fellow,' he said at last. 'It is true that you erred in your identification of this poor inoffensive old chap, as you call him, but that was understandable. As for his being killed by the man, or men, who killed Greville, that is probably true enough. But you have, in your own inimitable fashion, quite missed the really significant point.'

'Oh? And what is that?'

'Well, why do you think this Tromarty was in the wood last night in the first place? It was not for any truly nefarious purpose, you have said as much yourself, or at any rate you implied it, and I concur.'

'That's true. But yet he was following me, Holmes. I can swear to that. Wait, though. If he was not following me to do any sort of mischief –' I shook my head. 'I give it up, Holmes. Explain, if you will. If you can.'

'Oh, I fancy I can. He was curious, Watson. Nothing more elaborate than that. Greville, and then this lad, your namesake, both thought that something was amiss at the school. Why should Mr Tromarty not think the same? And then a mysterious "Mr Harris" arrives out of the blue, pretty clearly no school master – no offence, dear fellow – and starts asking some awkward questions, even claims an acquaintance with Sherlock Holmes and Dr John Watson!

What more natural than that Tromarty should at once suspect Harris of being implicated in some way in the general mystery? He was right enough in that, in a general sense. And so what more natural than that Tromarty should keep an alert eye on Harris? And what does Tromarty see? He sees Harris scuttling out at night, and lurking in the ruins of the old abbey!'

'He followed me for no better reason? Or worse reason?'

'I think not, Watson.'

'But why was he killed?' I asked, puzzled.

'Watson, Watson! You did not kill him, I take it?'

'Really, Holmes!'

'Well, then, that narrows the matter down somewhat, does it not?' And Holmes lit his pipe with great care.

I thought a moment, then had to lean against a tree trunk for support. 'You mean that the murderer thought it was me?'

Holmes nodded. 'That is exactly what I mean, Watson. You were evidently getting too close to the truth, and the killer wanted you out of the way. Only he got the wrong man. That is my reading of it.'

'Well, Holmes, if you are right, then that scarcely cheers me up to any great extent. I now feel that I am indeed to blame for Tromarty's death.'

'Oh, that is sheer nonsense. You are not to blame for his being curious. Curiosity killed the cat, you know, Watson. And besides, it is merely my surmise that he was killed in error. Tromarty had, when all is said and done, been at the Abbey School much longer than you have, and he may well have uncovered something you have not. You said, I believe, that he had visited the ruins, or the spinney, at any rate, before last night?'

'Indeed.'

'Well, then. That earlier visit cannot have been connected with your presence, can it? Perhaps the earlier visit was the result of an earlier suspicion that something was amiss. His suspicions of you, if any, may have been a part of the overall sense of unease which he felt. In that event, Tromarty's death may very well not have been accidental. You may not have been the intended victim. Tromarty may in fact have uncovered something, a vital clue, and been killed to prevent his disclosing what he knew.'

'H'mm, that's true. You're not merely saying that to salve my conscience, though?'

Holmes smiled grimly. 'I fancy that you know me better than that, Doctor.'

'If that were so, it's a pity I didn't talk to him, find out what he knew.'

'But it is all surmise, and he may have known nothing. No, I agree that it is sad, and I accept that it gives us both an extra incentive to find the killer, but you are no more to blame than I am for sending you here. Or at any rate you are not to blame for his death,' he added, sighing as he gazed at the spot where I had stumbled over poor Tromarty the previous night. 'Why the devil could you not leave him there?' he complained.

'Holmes! It was cold, beginning to snow, we could not leave the poor fellow out in all that filthy weather.'

'Well at least you could have limited the number of spectators. The ground was wet, soft, ideal for taking an impression of a foot mark. As indeed it has; I see here the footprints of a couple of hundred boys, a dozen masters and a score of policemen.' He shook his head and sighed again.

'Don't be ridiculous, Holmes.' I looked at the muddy

soil, all churned up by the feet of those who had taken Tromarty from the spinney. 'I agree that it is a trifle confused, but then that could be said with equal truth of events in general last night. I am truly sorry, Holmes.'

'Ah, well, no great harm done, Doctor. But this nonsense has gone on quite long enough, I think.'

'I agree.'

'Where is our starting point, though?' asked Holmes, setting off back through the spinney.

'I don't know. This secret society, perhaps?'

'Ah, yes, the secret society. You have no details of that, I gather?'

'Only heard of its existence last night, Holmes.'

'At that, you did better than I did!' Holmes stopped at the ruins, and indicated a more substantial piece of masonry than the rest. A stout, and relatively new, wooden door stood in the middle of the stonework. Holmes lifted the modern padlock which held the door shut. 'H'mm. This has not been opened recently, at any rate.' He produced a key. 'I obtained this from the head this morning, despite his reluctance. Shall we see what the fuss is about?'

He turned the key in the padlock with some difficulty. 'As I thought, it has not been oiled, or opened, lately.' He pulled the door aside, and produced a candle and match. 'Shall I go first?'

I followed him down a narrow, steep flight of steps. 'Original stairs, Holmes?'

'I imagine so.' He held the candle up, to illuminate a vaulted cellar. 'Impressive, Watson. But unoccupied, and, judging by the dust, hasn't been visited for some considerable time.'

'Yes, quite reminds one of your rooms. Graves – the

deputy head – said that no-one had been down here recently. Though I rather took the liberty of doubting him.'

'Ah, you did well not to take too much for granted. But I think he spoke the truth.'

'But the rumours about the ruins, Holmes?'

'I imagine they were originally more or less naturally occurring,' said he, leading the way up the stairs and out into the open. 'Then, of course, whoever is behind all this would encourage such tales, as a diversion, a red herring.'

'I see! Whilst I, and others, are wondering, and indeed wandering, about the ruins, we are not bothering to look elsewhere. Ingenious.'

Holmes nodded, and locked the door carefully. 'And effective. For I take it you have no idea as to where else to start looking?'

I shook my head. 'Afraid not, Holmes. The only thing I can suggest is a laborious questioning of everyone at the school.'

He groaned.

'I know,' I said quickly, 'it'll takes ages. But what alternative is there? Especially now you have arrived on the scene.'

'Oh?'

'I mean, it was bad enough when it was just me, but the culprit will be even more on his guard now you're here.'

Holmes thought. 'He may, but then he may believe that he has eliminated the danger. That rather depends –' and he broke off and stared at me in silence for a time, then shrugged his shoulders. 'As you say, Watson, question and answer it must be, now. Our starting point must be the boys to whom you have already spoken, Watson Minor and Major, and this Edmonds, was it?'

'Yes. It was the elder Watson and a boy called Meade

who were out here last night, so it might be as well to start with them. They may have seen something important.'

'Would they not say as much last night?'

'It was all very confused, Holmes.'

'I see. In that case we had best see them at once, before they quite forget what happened.' And he cast a final look at the ruins before setting back to the main school building, now all quiet for it was mid-morning.

We had decided that my own rooms would form our joint headquarters for the conduct of the investigation, and there we went. Holmes had, as I say, secured the rather reluctant co-operation of Dr Longton, who had promised that masters and boys alike should answer any of our questions. Holmes now sent the porter, recruited as a temporary messenger and confederate, to fetch Watson Major and Meade, although it was in the very middle of a lesson. They showed, I must say, no great distress at the interruption. Holmes waved them to chairs, and dismissed the porter, who was somewhat inclined to linger, saying that we should not hesitate to call upon him again were it necessary.

Holmes smiled at the two boys. He took out his pipe, glanced at the boys, sighed, and put the pipe away again. 'Now,' said he, 'why were you following Dr Watson last night?'

It was Watson Major who answered. 'Sheer nosiness, sir,' he said frankly. 'We suspected something was afoot, have done for a while, now, and when we saw Mr Harris – Dr Watson, that is to say – heading for the old ruins, well, we simply couldn't resist following.'

'I see. How came you to see Dr Watson, though? Would you, should you, for that matter, not have been at your studies?' asked Holmes.

Watson Major flushed. 'It was getting towards lights out, sir, so we had done our prep and what have you. We happened to be outside –'

'Oh?'

'Merely for a breath of fresh air,' explained Watson Major.

'And perhaps a cigar?' I suggested.

The looks on the faces of the two boys showed that this was not far off the mark. Holmes regarded me with something like admiration. 'Remarkable, Watson!'

'Oh, merely a knowledge of the youthful mentality, Holmes. So, you saw me, and followed? But did you also see Mr Tromarty?'

Watson Major nodded. 'We were just about to set off after you, sir, when Meade here spotted old – spotted poor Mr Tromarty. He said, or I did, "This looks like fun", or something of the sort. Of course, when we saw him obviously following you, that made us quite determined to follow, to see what was going on.' He broke off, and shook his head. ' "Fun", we thought,' he added. 'In the event, of course –'

'I was very glad you were there,' I told them. 'I would not have liked to be on my own when I found Mr Tromarty there.'

'Tell me,' said Holmes, 'you saw the Doctor here, and you saw Mr Tromarty. Did you happen to see or hear anyone else last night?'

'No, sir. But there must have been someone else,' said Watson Major, 'because we had absolutely nothing to do with poor Mr Tromarty's death, I promise you that!'

'No, no, we do not suggest any such thing,' said Holmes. 'But you have no idea as to who the mysterious third party may have been?'

'It was pretty dark, sir,' said Meade. 'And we, or I, at any rate, imagined all sorts of noises in the wood.'

'Yes,' said Watson Major, 'what with the dark, and the excitement, one could fancy all sorts of hobgoblins out there. In fact, I'm sure I heard a thud or thump, just before – just before we found Dr Watson here.'

'Yes, I thought I'd heard something of that sort, too,' I said.

'Was that –' and Meade broke off.

'It very likely was,' I said. 'The proverbial blunt instrument, I fancy, from the injuries I saw. A sock filled with sand would do it. Of course, if it had been me, I might have stood a chance, but Mr Tromarty was so very old and frail, by comparison. Poor chap.'

'Yes,' said Meade thoughtfully. 'I never thought of him like that, you know, sir. If anything, he was a bit of a joke with us, a figure of fun. Sad, really. Makes you think, doesn't it, sir?'

'Profound though these sentiments are,' said Holmes, 'this is not getting us any nearer to identifying Mr Tromarty's murderer. My next question is just this: what do you know of any secret society or societies in the school?'

Watson Major said, 'Only what I told Dr Watson last night, sir. I think there's such a thing, but I'm not a member of it if there is, so I can't say for sure.'

'Meade?'

Meade hesitated. 'I'd have to say the same as Watson, sir.'

'Nothing more?' Holmes had clearly spotted the hesitation just as I had.

'Well, sir, I don't know if this is the sort of thing you mean, or if it would matter, but I do know that the head sometimes gives certain boys special coaching.'

'Oh?'

'Does he?' said Watson Major, with some surprise. 'I've never heard of anything like that.'

Meade flushed. 'I only know because I had a bit of an upset with my Latin a year or so back. Long – I mean, Dr Longton, gave me a few lessons on my own, put me on the right track, as it were.'

'I never knew that,' said Watson Major again.

'Not the sort of thing a chap talks about, is it, old fellow?' mumbled Meade. 'But it's a fact, and I know that the head has done the same sort of thing with some of the other chaps. Particularly the ones from overseas, India and what have you.'

Holmes shook his head. 'I hardly think that would qualify as a secret society,' he said, 'but I appreciate your candour, Mr Meade. And I assure you that your revelations will go no further.' He glanced at Watson Major.

'Oh, absolutely, absolutely,' said Watson Major, turning a brick red. 'Not that hot at Latin myself, come to that.'

'Who is?' I asked.

'I am a trifle rusty myself these days,' said Holmes with a laugh. He stood up. 'Well, Mr Watson, Mr Meade, thank you for your help. I shall not keep you from your studies any longer,' and he shook hands with the two boys and showed them out.

'No new clues there, Holmes,' I said.

'You discount what Meade said?'

'Not exactly a secret society, is it? And besides, one could hardly suspect Dr Longton of being involved in anything underhand!'

'Could one not?'

'Really, Holmes!'

'You would attach no importance to Meade's statement that Dr Longton has given special attention to the foreign students?'

'Most probably he sees it as part of his job, to make them welcome over here. Nothing odd in that, Holmes, nothing odd at all. And again, some of them probably have difficulty speaking English, it being a foreign language to them. Anyway,' I went on, getting to my feet, 'the simplest thing is to ask Dr Longton about it. He should be in his study, and it's better to talk to him than to take the boys away from their classes with no real notion of what we want to ask them.'

'You are right, as usual,' said Holmes.

As I opened the door, a thought struck me. 'By the way, Holmes, speaking of this secret society, so-called, young Watson there told me that he thought Lord Whitechurch may have been approached to join it. He said as much last night, but in all the excitement I quite forgot about it.'

'That is interesting.'

'You think it may be significant? Is the Whitechurch business part and parcel of the murder, d'you think?'

'Well, I think that a boy who did *not* join a secret society may perhaps be more disposed to talk about it than a boy who did, and who is governed by its rules and his own boyish notion of honour, Watson.' He found a piece of paper and a pencil, and scribbled a note. 'I think I shall ask the porter to send a telegram to the duke, and ask him to bring Lord Whitechurch here. Not to the school, perhaps, but there is an inn of sorts in the village, which would serve for a night or so. Thank you, Watson, that may be the clue we seek.'

'Oh, glad to help, Holmes. And Dr Longton?'

'Yes, we shall interview him, too. Five minutes, Doctor, and I shall be with you,' and Holmes vanished, presumably to find the porter and dispatch his telegram. He returned within the time he had specified, and we went off together to Dr Longton's study.

Carstairs glanced up as we entered the outer office. 'Solved the murder?' he asked cheerfully.

'I have hopes that I shall,' answered Holmes with some asperity. 'Would it be convenient to see Dr Longton just now?'

'I'll see.' Carstairs tapped on the inner door, put his head round it, and spoke briefly, before standing back to usher us into Dr Longton's room.

Dr Longton rose to greet us, a look of curiosity on his face. 'Gentlemen? You wish to see me?'

'It is nothing very serious,' said Holmes. 'I merely wished to ask if you sometimes give special coaching to certain boys?'

'Oh, is that all!' Dr Longton sat back, laughing. 'I don't imagine that there is a headmaster worthy of the name who does not, sir. Yes, when we see a boy in difficulties with his studies, the master who takes the subject concerned, or the boy's form master, or Mr Graves, or I, or any combination of those, set to work to correct matters as much as we are able. When the matter is of a more personal nature, of course, then the form master or I myself would be the one to deal with it.'

'And do such personal difficulties arise frequently?' asked Holmes.

'I imagine that we are no better or worse in that regard than any other boarding school,' said Dr Longton. 'There are inevitable family matters, bereavement, bankruptcy, and the like. In one memorable instance, I had to inform a lad that he was now King of his country, his father having met his death at the hands of an assassin.'

'Yes, I see. You perhaps have more occasion to deal in this way with the foreign students?'

'I think perhaps I do. Their being so very far from home, in some cases, makes it additionally difficult. When the boy's family is here in England, of course, then the boy can return home, should the need arise. But when the boy's home is in Delhi or Bombay, then I am very much in *loco parentis*, and I naturally try to act accordingly.'

'I quite understand.' Holmes was at a temporary loss, I could tell. He stood up. 'I am very sorry to have troubled you,' he said.

'Oh, no trouble.' Dr Longton, clearly wondering what it had all been about, showed us to the door. Carstairs nodded a farewell as we passed him.

In the corridor, Holmes paused a moment, then shrugged his shoulders. 'I need to think, Watson,' he told me. 'Perhaps a walk in the fields would clear our heads?' And without bothering to return for a coat or hat, he led the way outside.

EIGHT

'That didn't get us very far,' I said, as Holmes led the way across the playing fields at a smart pace.

'No?'

'Well, did it?'

'It rather hinges,' said Holmes didactically, 'on our definition of the term "secret society". Now, such an organization might be nothing more sinister than a few boys who enjoy raiding the school pantry under cover of darkness, or who collect butterflies, or birds' eggs, or postage stamps, or who fancy themselves as pirates, or whatever little boys get up to these days. And it may indeed be that this secret society, of which we have heard hints but nothing more substantial, is nothing more sinister than that. But suppose for a moment that a determined man, a man who had no love for England, were to desire to influence world affairs to England's detriment. There are several ways in which he might choose to achieve his objects, but surely one of the best ways would be to influence the hearts and minds of the boys who will become England's rulers, her statesmen? Do the Jesuits not have a saying to the effect that if they have the child for its first five years, it will be theirs for the rest of its life?'

'And you honestly think Dr Longton is up to something of the kind?' I asked, with a good deal of scepticism.

'Well, someone is "up to" something at the school, Watson.

The murder of Mr Tromarty alone proves that, even if we accept the Whitechurch affair and the death of Greville as being sheer coincidence.'

'That's true,' I admitted.

'Let us suppose – a supposition only, a working hypothesis, an intellectual device – let us suppose that Dr Longton is an agent of a foreign power, an unfriendly foreign power. Under the pretext of extra coaching he selects certain boys, whose fathers are, let us say, diplomatists, Cabinet Ministers, and what have you. He will not use any crude methods, to be sure, but there are other ways to influence a boy. Flattery, or the old standby, "world peace", say, or "the brotherhood of man". He persuades them that if there were no diplomatic secrets, there will be no wars, no spies, no more hatred. He suggests that they keep alert when they return home for the holidays, report anything they overhear –'

'Holmes!'

He ignored me. 'Or again, he talks to some of the Indian princes. Very likely they have divided loyalties to begin with. You or I would, I think, resent an invading force occupying our country, so why should these boys not feel the same? Dr Longton suggests that one way to remove the British presence in India might be to conclude some treaty with Russia –'

'Really, Holmes!' I paused. 'Russia?'

'You know Russian ambitions with regard to India as well as I do. These lads will one day be rulers of provinces, men whose goodwill is essential if Britain is to retain her influence on the subcontinent. Russia, yes, or others. Nearer home, Germany has her own colonial ambitions.'

'Yes, indeed. Herr Wieland was saying much the same thing the other day.'

'Was he, indeed?'

'Oh, but you can't suspect Wieland! Why, he climbs mountains, Holmes.'

'An unimpeachable recommendation, to be sure.'

'But how would Wieland fit in with this theory about Dr Longton, then?'

'I cannot say. Remember that it is merely a theory, a speculative possibility. Perhaps Longton is innocent, and Herr Wieland is behind it all?'

'No, never. Although I did wonder about him, you know. But then if he were, would he not rather pretend to be sympathetic to England, instead of harping on about German expansion?'

'Ah, a fool might seek to conceal his sympathies by going to the opposite extreme, but a clever man might use other methods. After all, if he is known as a fervent German patriot, he gains a certain reputation for eccentricity in that regard, does he not? And eccentrics are usually considered harmless. Remember, it is not the man who boasts loudest of his conquests whom other men are afraid to leave alone with their wives! Again, any slip Wieland might make, a word in the wrong place, say, would be concealed by the fact that he is known to have extreme views, such things are expected of him.'

'The double bluff, you mean?'

'If that is the correct literary term,' said Holmes. He nodded down the lane towards the little village. 'It might be as well if we enquired at the inn about rooms for the duke,' he said. 'And I suggest we take our luncheon there, too, for that will avoid any embarrassment.'

I concurred, for I too had not relished the idea of sitting down to the table with my erstwhile colleagues; it was quite bad enough to have deceived them in the way that I had. We took our humble luncheon at the inn, then, and Holmes reserved a couple of rooms for the following day, using the name of Harris, which he appeared to have forgotten was my old alias.

The meal over, we sat in the inn's little parlour, smoking our pipes and talking over the case. 'I am reluctant to return to the school just at the moment,' said Holmes frankly. 'They will expect some action from us, and I have not the least idea as to how to proceed.'

'Despite your elaborate theory about the secret society?' I could not help asking.

Holmes laughed. 'It is as elaborate as one could wish,' he said, 'and if correct it would explain just about everything. The problem is, there is no means of saying if it is correct.'

'Well, then, let us examine such facts as we know *are* correct. Let us take the murder of Tromarty, to start with, and consider it, not as part of an overall mystery at the school, but merely as a problem in its own right. Study it like any other case that might be brought to our attention, Holmes. We agree that is was no boy who killed him?'

Holmes frowned. 'One of the older boys, perhaps? But no, again as a working hypothesis only, it was a man.'

'And a master at the school? The balance of probability says that it must be so.'

'Agreed.'

'There we are! Check their whereabouts last night, I know the exact time, and we may be able to eliminate or incriminate.'

'Excellent, Watson! Now, the second item, namely the death of Greville. Anything there?'

'Oh, I forgot to tell you; the excitement last night, you know, Holmes. Carstairs met him just before he died.'

'Indeed? Carstairs?'

'Yes, apparently Greville was in a very nervous frame of mind.' And I went on to tell Holmes what Carstairs had told me. 'He should by rights have spoken up at the inquest,' I concluded, 'but you can see why he kept quiet.'

'Indeed. Of course, had you not been quite so alert, he might never have spoken up. For the same excellent reason, of course. Or another reason, perhaps not quite so excellent, I wonder?' He stared at the grimy panelling for a long time. 'Now, of course, matters are somewhat altered. Yes, it would –' and he stopped, and made a great show of lighting his pipe.

'Holmes?'

'Sorry, Watson, merely musing aloud. Yes, if Greville did not fall, then he was pushed, and a young fellow like Carstairs would be an ideal candidate for the man who did the pushing.'

'I think you're wrong, Holmes. If he had anything to hide, he'd have hidden it. He was quite frank with me, even as to his motive for originally concealing the fact that he met Greville. But I agree that it would need a strong man, especially if Greville were unconscious, let us say, or put up a struggle, when he was taken up the tower. That would appear to eliminate Monsieur Legrand, who is too old and weak. And Donaldson, for the same reason.'

'Unless one or both were acting in concert with a younger man? Or some of the older boys? I know the suggestion is repellent, but if we postulate an evil society, we must allow for that possibility.'

'Like the Assassins, you mean? Or the Thugs?' I shuddered. 'I hardly like to think of schoolboys behaving in that fashion, Holmes. But then some of them are young men, so it is perhaps not so very fanciful.'

Holmes knocked out his pipe on the table. 'Our best course is, as you say, to ask where the masters were last night,' he said. 'That should enable us to limit our enquiries.' And he called the landlord, paid our modest reckoning, and led the way outside.

By the time we reached the school, the first lesson of the afternoon was under way. Holmes seemed disposed to fret at this, but I insisted that we should not interrupt the school curriculum any more than necessary. We could, I told him, question the masters when the day's duties were over.

'We can talk to Carstairs, at any rate,' he muttered. 'And the head, too.' He led the way to Carstairs's office, tapped on the door and went in.

'Hullo!' said Carstairs. 'Want to see Dr Longton again? He's in, but I'll have to ask if he's busy.'

'We wanted a word with both of you,' said Holmes.

'Oh? Sounds serious.'

'Not at all. I merely wished to ask where you were last night, at, say, five o'clock?'

'Oh, is that all?' Carstairs looked relieved. 'I was in my own rooms, as a matter of fact.'

'Alone?'

'No, I was talking to Mr Donaldson. Or he was talking to me, rather. He has a bit of a bee in his bonnet about the old organ, you know, wants to restore it and so forth. Dr Watson will tell you the same. Anyway, he was wanting to ask me whether funds would permit of his beginning the restoration work this term or not. Ask him, if you like.'

'Thank you,' said Holmes. 'Do they, by the way?'

'I'm sorry?'

'Do funds permit a beginning on the restoration work?'

'Lord, I don't know!' Carstairs laughed aloud. 'That's not up to me, you know. As I told him, but he didn't listen. Just went on about his pet undertaking, how much better morning prayers would be if the organ were restored, all that sort of thing. Truth to tell, I didn't really listen most of the time.'

'I see. Well, perhaps we might see Dr Longton, if it is not inconvenient?'

'Of course.' As before, Carstairs tapped on the inner door, spoke briefly to the headmaster, and showed us in.

'Well, gentlemen?' Dr Longton's words were civil enough, but there was a tinge of impatience in his tone.

'It is a small matter,' said Holmes. 'We merely wish to eliminate all the members of staff from our enquiries by determining where they may have been at five o'clock last night.'

'You suspect me?'

Holmes raised a hand. 'Merely a matter of form, sir, I assure you.'

'Well, then, I was in here, talking to the chairman of the school governors. I can give you his name and address, if you think it necessary?'

'No, sir, it will not be necessary,' said Holmes. He stood up and smiled. 'By giving the lead so readily in this respect, you have assisted us considerably, for the rest of the staff will not now refuse to answer us,' he said.

'I see. Pleased to help in any way, of course,' said Dr Longton, somewhat mollified.

Holmes nodded a farewell, and we returned to our rooms. The fire had been lit, and the place was pleasantly warm.

Holmes curled up in a chair, and took out his pipe. 'With your permission,' he said, 'I shall think over what we have achieved so far. Not that it will take very long,' he added cynically. 'And we can resume our questions when the rest of the masters have finished the day's teaching.'

I nodded, and set off for the bedroom to find a book which I had brought with me, for there was no mistaking Holmes's meaning; he wanted to be allowed to muse in silence. As I reached the inner door I recollected that I had been reading the book the day before, and had left it on a little table by the outer door. I retraced my steps, then, but when I got to the table I forgot about the book, for there lay a medium sized parcel, wrapped in brown paper and addressed in pencil to 'Dr John Watson, The Abbey School.'

Considerably puzzled, I picked it up, and tore off the outer wrapper, to reveal a box of twenty-five Havana cigars. I could not repress a laugh.

'What have you there, Watson?'

'Cigars, Holmes. A decent brand, too. I fancy I could name the two little rascals who bought these!'

'Indeed?'

'Yes, Holmes. Caught young Watson and his pal smoking some revolting things the night before last, and gave them a couple of decent smokes. Not that they agreed with 'em, mind you.'

'And you think they have bought these as a way of thanking you?'

'Can't see why anyone else would send me cigars, Holmes,' I said, wondering what he was talking about.

'I hardly think the village shop stocks this particular brand,' he said.

'No, I suppose not. They most likely ordered them from

London, from the merchants used by one of their fathers, or something.'

'There is no postmark. The address, you see, is in capitals.'

'The shopman, Holmes!'

'And the absence of a postmark?'

'Sent by carrier, dear chap!'

'And when did they learn that you were not Mr Harris, but Dr Watson?'

'Oh.'

Very gently, Holmes took the box from my hand, and examined it closely. 'Have the goodness to open the window, Watson.'

No less puzzled than before, I did as he asked.

'Anyone out there?'

'No-one at all, Holmes.'

'Then stand clear.' And before I could stop him, or even ask what he proposed, he had thrown the box through the open window! I watched as it sailed in a neat arc, to land in the very centre of the empty quadrangle. As it struck the ground, it exploded with a bang that broke a couple of ground floor windows.

NINE

'The old exploding cigar trick, eh, Holmes?' was the best I could manage as I leaned for support against the window sill.

'Remarkable, Watson,' he said with some admiration. 'Most men would not be able to treat so grave a matter quite so lightly. I think we had better examine the wrapper of your curious parcel more closely.'

'And I think I had better check to see if anyone was hurt in the blast, Holmes.'

'Oh, do you think so?' Holmes thought for a moment, then nodded. 'I am sorry, Watson. You are right, of course, although I do not think any harm has been done.' If he seemed a touch disappointed at the prospect of not being able to pursue his own line immediately, it was merely a touch, and I ignored this and made my way down to the ground floor. As you may imagine, the explosion had not gone entirely unremarked. Boys and masters alike were wandering into the quadrangle, and there was much speculation as to what exactly had happened. But there was no sort of panic, and no injuries beyond the predictable nervous shock experienced by those who had been in the classrooms nearest the blast. One or two boys had been obliged to brush bits of glass from their desks, or their persons, but although the explosion had sufficient force to break a couple of windows it had been insufficient to propel the glass fragments at a truly dangerous speed.

When once I had found that my medical skills were not required, I very naturally became the focus of attention with regard to what had happened. I tried to fend off the many questions addressed to me – for it was assumed that the occurrence was in some way connected with Holmes and me – and I was relieved when Holmes strolled casually up and dismissed the whole thing with an airy wave of his hand, and some story about a chemical experiment that had not worked out entirely as intended. With this excuse, pathetic though it patently was, the enquirers had to be satisfied.

Holmes nodded to me to join him. He sought out the porter, who was expressing some incoherent views as to just what had happened, and steered him to a quieter spot.

'Bit of a rum do, this, sir,' ventured the porter.

'It is indeed. Tell me,' said Holmes, producing the brown paper wrapper from his pocket, 'was it you who left a parcel for Dr Watson in his rooms?'

The man hesitated, then nodded. 'But 'twas the doctor himself gave it me, sir,' he added.

'The doctor? You mean Dr Longton?'

The porter nodded.

'Dr Longton brought the parcel to you?' I asked, unable to believe that such was the case.

'No, sir. I had occasion to go along to Dr Longton's room, a small matter of reporting a little trouble with the main boiler in the kitchens. Trouble is, you see, that boiler is near as old as the school itself, and –'

'And Dr Longton gave you the parcel for Dr Watson here?' Holmes cut in.

'That 'e did, sir.'

'I see. Thank you.' Holmes nodded, and turned back to the crowd, which was now beginning to thin out slightly. Dr Longton was still there, though, looking not so much puzzled as angry at this further disturbance to the even tenor of the school's life. 'Dr Longton, may we have a word with you?'

'You may, sir, if it embraces some sort of apology for this disgraceful episode,' said Dr Longton.

Holmes regarded him severely. 'Watson and I have but narrowly escaped death or serious injury,' he said. 'There was some infernal machine contained in a purported box of cigars, which I understand you caused to be sent to the doctor's rooms?'

'Was that what caused the explosion, then?' Dr Longton's surprise was unfeigned, I was sure of that.

'It was, sir.'

'Well,' said Dr Longton, 'That casts a slightly different light upon matters. But I can assure you that I know nothing whatever about the parcel. It is true that I saw it upon Carstairs's desk after luncheon. In the ordinary way of things, I should simply have left it there, for Carstairs sees to the post and what have you as a rule, but, since the school porter chanced to call upon me about some minor domestic mishap, the details of which I cannot now even recall with any accuracy —'

'A complaint as to some old boiler, I think?' I ventured.

'Possibly so,' agreed Dr Longton. 'As I say, the porter was there, and Carstairs was not, so I indicated the parcel when the porter left, and asked him to be so kind as to deliver it.'

'I see. And where was Carstairs?' asked Holmes.

'He had gone to the bank immediately after luncheon, and not returned.'

'I see,' said Holmes again. 'And can you recall seeing the

parcel there before luncheon?'

'I cannot, sir. But then I may well not have noticed it, so I cannot say that it was not there earlier.'

'Is Carstairs back, do you know?'

'He was here somewhere.' Dr Longton looked round the quadrangle, now all but empty of sightseers. 'He has very likely returned to his duties, and with your permission I shall do the same.' And he nodded a farewell and set off back inside.

'We had better see Carstairs,' Holmes decided, 'although I do not expect that he will be able to tell us very much more.' And he followed Dr Longton at a discreet distance.

Carstairs was at his desk when we reached his office. He looked up and raised an eyebrow. 'A bit of a fuss there, what?' he said.

'Watson's life, and mine, have been put at risk by a device concealed in a cigar box,' said Holmes.

'Oh? Is that what the commotion was?'

'The cigar box was delivered to Watson after Dr Longton had seen it upon your desk.'

'Was it, by Jove? Well, it wasn't here before lunch, I promise you that.'

'You took your luncheon at the usual hour?'

Carstairs nodded. 'And then I had to go into the village, do some school business at the bank. You can ask Dr Longton, if you like.'

'Thank you, that will not be necessary. And there was no parcel here when you left, you say? You did not, I take it, see anyone outside when you went to your luncheon?'

'Lurking with a parcel under their arm? No, sir, I did not.' Carstairs frowned. 'Anyone might have left it here, though, for I have only just properly got back.'

'Did anyone know you were going to the bank?'

'Only Dr Longton. The porter sometimes goes with me, partly to act as an escort, and also to do some shopping or similar errands if needed, but the nature of today's business meant that I would be quite safe alone. But anyone might have left it in here, the parcel I mean, throughout the lunch interval. Once the meal itself is over, people drift off for a smoke, or a short walk, or a chat, you know.'

'H'mm.' I could tell that Holmes was far from satisfied. 'Thank you,' he told Carstairs, and then he ushered me out into the corridor and along to our rooms.

'Less than helpful,' I said.

'Indeed.'

'Shall we resume our questioning of the masters as to their whereabouts?' I asked him.

'I feel that it will probably be quite useless,' he answered shortly. Then he laughed, and threw his cigar case over to me. 'Those won't explode! You see, Watson, I fancy that our man, or men, will have a decent alibi,' he went on. 'After all, it was just after the conclusion of the day's work, so what more natural than that the teachers should be in their own rooms, having a bath, or a smoke, or just closing their eyes in their armchairs? It would be impossible to prove otherwise. And where two men claim to have been in one another's company, who is to say that they are not the men we seek, and that they have concocted the tale to rule themselves out as suspects? We are dealing with clever men, Watson. And dangerous men.'

'We might eliminate any who have a provable story, though.'

'That is true. We shall do what we can later.' Holmes

smoked thoughtfully in silence for a time. 'It does rather prove one thing, though. I had wondered if Tromarty might have been killed on purpose, to prevent his telling something he had found out. This attempt on both our lives makes it more likely that you were, in fact, the intended victim.'

'And now they – whoever "they" may be – want you out of the way as well. That will not make for a very pleasant time, Holmes, for they might very well decide to try again!'

'Yes, indeed. I think I might have a word with Dr Longton, explain that we shall take up our quarters in the village inn for a time. I imagine he will not be too sorry to see us go.' And Holmes left me for a few minutes, telling me on his return that all was arranged, and that we should leave once we had spoken to the rest of the masters.

We were then obliged to possess our souls in patience, or as much as we could decently summon up. I fretted somewhat, and would have taken a long walk to pass the time, but my nerves were rather shaken by the events of the afternoon, and I thought it safer to remain where I was. Holmes, of course, seemed completely indifferent to what had occurred, and curled up in an armchair with his pipe and his own thoughts.

After a couple of hours, which seemed to me more like a couple of weeks, the final bell sounded, and Holmes stood up with a grunt of satisfaction. 'We can get some work done, now,' he said, setting off at a good pace down the corridor.

We questioned each of the masters in turn. I do not propose to set down all the conversations, but our investigations may be summarized thus: Mr Reed could be eliminated, for he had talked to a couple of the villagers on his way home, and then the local doctor had called that evening regarding the Reeds's baby, which had some childish ailment. Herr Wieland said he had been talking to a couple of the older boys. 'We cannot cross him off, though?' I pointed out, 'for they might all three be involved.'

'H'mm. Agreed. By the same token, we cannot eliminate Dr Longton.'

'But he was with the chairman of the school governors!' I said.

'True, but what of that? If the older boys are suspect, then why should the chairman of the governors not be suspect as well? After all, if we can picture the respectable Dr Longton as being involved in some as yet undefined skullduggery, why should he not be in concert with the equally respectable chairman?'

'Unlikely, Holmes. Though I agree we must be careful. What of Donaldson and Carstairs? They were together, according to Carstairs.'

'According to Carstairs. Again, we must leave them on our list.'

And that, if you will believe me, was all the result of our questions! The other masters claimed, as Holmes had predicted, to have been alone in their individual rooms, with no witnesses to say yea or nay. Still, we had eliminated Reed, so I suppose it might be called progress of a kind.

Once this dismal work was concluded, Holmes and I took such essentials as we must and decamped for the village inn, where we spent but a poor evening. Holmes was not disposed to engage in idle talk, and I was reduced to playing a form of indoor skittles with an old fellow whose conversation, though sprightly enough in content, was somewhat impeded by his almost complete lack of teeth.

This did not, however, preclude his beating me at every game. All in all, I was not sorry when I could excuse myself and seek my bed.

I slept fitfully, my nerves shaken by the incident earlier that day, and I woke with a thick head and in no very sweet temper. The morning dragged intolerably, and it was with very considerable relief that I looked out of the inn door at half past eleven, to see a trap come to a halt, and a distinguished man step down, followed by a lad of twelve or thirteen.

Holmes hurried forward, rubbing his hands in glee. 'Thank you for taking the trouble to meet us here, Your Grace,' he said. 'And this, I take it, is Lord Whitechurch?'

The Duke of Greyminster nodded, and Holmes introduced me to our guests. 'If you would care to step inside,' said Holmes, 'we may be able to make some progress in our investigation.'

The duke and young Lord Whitechurch followed us inside, and Holmes said, 'We were unsure as to just when you would arrive, Your Grace, and so I took the liberty of reserving a couple of rooms.'

The duke glanced around with some dismay. 'I trust we may be able to conclude our business in time for us to take the train back this evening,' he said.

'As you wish. In that event, it would be as well if we got to work immediately,' said Holmes. 'It was Lord Whitechurch that I really wished to see. Your Grace, might I ask you to step into the other room for a few moments? I am sure the landlord can provide a glass of beer, or a cup of coffee, should you wish it.'

The duke looked surprised, then nodded and left us. 'Now, my lord,' said Holmes, 'I know this is a painful topic, but I must ask you one or two questions about the Abbey

School.'

Lord Whitechurch had an air of self-assurance, but he looked a touch perturbed at this.

Holmes shook his head. 'I promise that it will not be anything very troublesome,' said he. 'Now, am I right in thinking that you were asked to join some sort of secret society, just before your unfortunate expulsion?'

The lad started at this. 'I don't know how you knew, sir,' he told Holmes, 'but, yes, you are quite right.'

'And you declined the invitation?'

'Yes, sir.'

'May I ask why?'

Young Lord Whitechurch thought a moment. 'It's hard to define exactly, sir,' he said at last. 'I just felt that something wasn't quite right, if you follow me.'

'Yes, an impression that all was not above board?' asked Holmes.

Lord Whitechurch nodded.

'You asked the elder Watson brother what he thought, I gather?'

'Yes, sir. He said it was fine to join a club or society or what have you, so long as you were sure that it was appropriate for you. And I thought this one wasn't.'

'May I ask if there was anything more substantial than your intuitive aversion? Were you told the objects of the society, say?'

'Not as such, sir. I was just told that I had been chosen, nominated, to be a member, and that it was a great honour which I couldn't refuse.'

'Ah! Was it a master who told you this, or one of your fellow pupils?'

'One of the older boys, sir.'

'And yet you did refuse?'

'Yes, sir. I promised to think about it, and give my answer later that day. That was when I asked Watson Major, and I didn't think it was right for me, and so I said "no, thank you".'

'And their reaction?'

Lord Whitechurch smiled, without humour. 'Well, sir, the boy who'd told me, and who I said "no" to, just said, "'you can't refuse", sir. But I said I did refuse, and he went off.'

'And shortly after that you were accused of theft and expelled?'

Lord Whitechurch winced, and gazed at the floor. 'Yes, sir.'

'Did you steal that money?'

'No, sir.'

'I believe you,' said Holmes. 'I am sorry now that I did not listen to your father, the duke. Had I taken his case – your case – things might have been very different. Tell me,' he added in a more businesslike tone, 'who was the leading light in this society? One of the masters, I presume?'

'Yes, sir.'

'Well, then, who?'

'Mr Donaldson, sir.'

'What, the old music teacher?'

Lord Whitechurch nodded.

'Thank you,' said Holmes. 'Come along, Watson.'

TEN

'Old Mr Donaldson?' I said, as Holmes and I hurried through the village and back to the school. 'I could never imagine his being involved in anything criminal, Holmes. The lad means well; I am certain he told no more nor less than the truth, but he very probably got it wrong, and old Donaldson probably runs a glee club. They most likely sing polyphonic motets or whatever people do sing.'

Holmes laughed mirthlessly. 'You may well be right, Watson. In that event, we can eliminate Donaldson from our list of suspects.'

We turned in through the school gate, nodding to our old friend the porter as we passed him. Holmes pulled out his watch. 'I take it they will be at luncheon?' he said.

'Just finished, I should think.' I led the way to the dining hall, but before we could reach it, we encountered a throng of boys going the other way, having evidently finished their meal, as I had predicted. 'Have you seen Mr Donaldson?' I asked the nearest boys.

'Just left the hall, sir,' came the reply.

'Probably in his rooms, Holmes.' And I changed direction and set off for Donaldson's rooms.

As we reached the top of the staircase and turned the corner into the corridor which housed the rooms we sought, I caught sight of Donaldson himself, at the far end of the corridor, about to open the door of his study. Without thinking, I called out his name. Holmes, at my side, gave a little murmur of annoyance, while Donaldson, evidently startled, glanced along the corridor at us, then hastily went into his rooms.

'Come along, Watson!' Holmes set off down the corridor.

'No need to hurry, Holmes,' I told him. 'Unless his rooms are very different from my own, there is no way out save through the window, and I hardly think –' I broke off as Donaldson emerged. I had no time to boast that I had been right, though, for in his hand Donaldson held a large and old-fashioned revolver.

Holmes grabbed my arm and pulled me into the nearest set of rooms. None too soon, either, for there came a crash of the gun being fired, and a splintering as the bullet struck the door jamb not a foot from where we stood.

'Rather looks as if we've got our man, Holmes,' said I.

'You scintillate, Watson.' Holmes moved towards the doorway. 'The question now becomes, can we take him safely, or has he some bolt-hole, some supplementary means of egress?' He cautiously put his head round the door. I feared that there might be another shot – who could say that Donaldson had not crept closer? – but there was nothing. 'He has gone,' said Holmes, leading the way back into the corridor. 'And he must have gone this way. Be careful though, for he is apparently a fair shot.'

The latter sentiment had already occurred to me, but it seemed pointless to say as much. 'Wait, though,' I said, as Holmes started off along the corridor. 'If I am correct, the stairs at the far end lead to a side door. By retracing our steps, we should cut him off.'

Holmes nodded, and I set off back the way we had come. We encountered one or two curious glances from such boys or masters as had heard the shot, but there were few of these, as most were still in the dining hall or outside. We reached the side door which I remembered, and I cautiously looked outside, to see the figure of Donaldson hurrying away across the rugby field. 'There he goes, Holmes. Do we follow?'

'We do, but with care, for he is still armed. Where's he off, do you think?'

'It rather looks as if he's heading for the old abbey ruins,' I said doubtfully. This was the case, although I had not the least idea as to why it should be so, nor do I know for certain to this day. Possibly he had some notion of hiding in the ruins; more likely it was mere coincidence, and he was simply running away from us wherever his feet took him. Be that as it may, Donaldson was going in the direction of the little wood which housed the old ruins.

At that moment, though, he was in the middle of the playing field, and if we were to follow we should have to go out in the open as well, and that was not exactly the safest of courses, all things considered. I hazarded this opinion to Holmes.

He threw a calculating glance at the distance between us and Donaldson. 'H'mm. Even I would not guarantee to hit my man at this range,' he said. 'But you are right, we must be careful.' And with a complete disregard for either of us, he ran to the lee of that same pavilion behind which I had caught the two cigar smokers not long before. Here Holmes paused, and looked carefully at our quarry. He frowned. 'Hullo! What's he up to now, d'you think?'

I circumspectly poked my head round the angle of the

wall, and looked where Holmes pointed. Donaldson, who had been running in that curious hit-and-miss fashion of a man who is totally unused to strenuous exercise, had stopped in his tracks. He was not, as one might have expected, looking back at any possible pursuer, but standing with a hand to his side. 'Stitch, most likely,' I said. 'Not used to running. I wonder if we could –' and I stopped, as Donaldson suddenly plunged forward full length on his face.

Holmes turned to me. 'Some trick, would you say?'

I shook my head. 'Hard to say. I'd guess not, not out in the open like that. After all, a couple of minutes more and he'd have been in the shelter of the wood.'

'I concur.' Holmes produced his own revolver. 'Just in case, though.' And he set off at a run, the pistol held out ready to fire should it indeed prove to be some stratagem on Donaldson's part.

There was no stratagem, though. As I had thought, Donaldson must have been unused to exercise, and more particularly to the heavy work we had imposed upon him. To be brief, when I examined him I found that his heart had given out. He was beyond the aid of any doctor. I looked at Holmes, and shook my head.

'H'mm. Well, Watson, in a way this simplifies matters.'

'Flight being proof of guilt, you mean?' I asked, straightening up from the body. 'Not to speak of shooting at us!'

'Just so. But then I should have wished to ask Donaldson – if that was his real name – a few questions.'

'Indeed, Holmes. For one thing, this weak old fellow could hardly have killed a young chap like Greville. And I wouldn't have thought that he could even use a bludgeon on Tromarty.'

'No, again I agree with you.' Holmes frowned.

'Carstairs said that Donaldson was with him when Tromarty was killed,' I suggested.

'He did. Now, Donaldson may have been establishing an alibi. Or –'

'Or Carstairs was lying?'

Holmes nodded. 'We shall have to report this anyway,' he said, indicating Donaldson's body. He removed his coat, and laid it over the corpse. 'We may as well talk to Carstairs at the same time.' He turned towards the school.

'That will be easy, for here is the man himself,' I said, gesturing towards the far side of the playing field, where Carstairs was indeed making his way towards us at a good pace.

Holmes came to a full stop, and we waited until Carstairs, flushed and breathless, reached us. 'What's all the commotion?' asked Carstairs, glancing at the mortal remains hidden by Holmes's coat.

'Donaldson,' said Holmes shortly. 'He was one of the men we sought. His heart was unequal to the strain, but fortunately he did not die immediately.'

Before I could contradict this, Carstairs had shoved me violently into Holmes, and the two of us crashed to the ground. Carstairs himself took to his heels, heading back towards the school.

Holmes was the first to get up, and he wasted a moment or two giving me a hand. 'He should not get far, though,' he told me, as we set off at a run.

'Is the range too great for a shot?' I asked him.

'I want him alive if possible. There are too many questions unanswered.'

'Such as how many more of them are involved?'

Holmes gave a short laugh. 'He seems to be making for

the school buildings. In which case, we should be able to catch him.'

Carstairs was by this time almost at the main door of the school. I have told you that this door led to a short passage-way which opened on to the main assembly hall and so forth. Now, it was just after the luncheon interval, and, either because they had heard the shot or seen some unusual activity, or simply because they wanted a breath of fresh air, a small group of masters was making its way out from the main building, and Carstairs's way inside was therefore blocked.

I called out something incoherent, and the man in the lead, Herr Wieland, sensing that something was amiss, held his arms out as a further barrier to Carstairs's progress. Carstairs slowed his headlong flight, half turned, for all the world like a hare that jinks to elude the hounds, then seemed to vanish actually within the doorway.

'The tower!' cried Holmes, slowing down momentarily. He laughed. 'We have him now, Watson.'

'I thought that the door had been locked?' I mumbled churlishly. 'Should have been locked.'

'Ah, he very likely has a key, though. He could not rely upon the porter's faulty memory, could he? That was one point which worried me, though this is hardly the time to discuss loose ends.' We had arrived at the door now, and Holmes, ignoring the questions of the puzzled little group, paused to consider his best course.

'Hardly matters, Holmes,' I pointed out. 'He cannot get out now, so we need not worry too much.'

'H'mm. We do not know if he is armed, though. A determined man might do a good deal of damage, even with a small pistol. I think we had best pursue him at once.'

And with a word to the others to keep the boys well away, and to take similar evasive action on their own account, Holmes gripped my arm and led me inside the base of the tower.

I confess that I have been more cheerful towards the conclusion of an investigation. True, one does not – unless his pupils be very unruly – expect a schoolmaster to walk around with a revolver swinging from his hip in the manner of the Sagebrush Kid, or some other of the Wild West Heroes of the penny dreadfuls; but then Donaldson had been armed, and had not hesitated to shoot at us. What was there to say that Carstairs might not be similarly provided with a pistol? And he had the advantage of height, he was above us looking down! As we made our way slowly up the winding iron stair, I expected at any moment to hear the crash of a pistol shot ring out in the confined space. Holmes must have had similar unpalatable thoughts, for I saw him take out his own revolver and check the chambers.

There was no shot, though. We reached the topmost landing without incident, to see Carstairs lounging against the window, presumably that through which Greville had passed earlier, smoking a cigarette with no appearance of concern. As we started towards him, he threw the window open, and held up a hand, as if in warning. 'It was a valiant effort,' he said. 'Ours, I mean. Although your own was none too dusty, Doctor, nor yours, Mr Holmes. I give you best.' He threw his cigarette away. 'However, you must excuse me. The penalty for treason is death, and I prefer to choose my own time, and indeed manner.'

'It may not come to that,' said Holmes suavely.

'Oh, I think it would, you know. In any event, the penalty for murder is the same, so it is six of one, half a dozen of the other, as my old nurse used to say. The murders, Tromarty, Greville, must be laid to my account, by the by. Not that it matters, I imagine.'

'But –' Holmes leaped forward, but he was just too late. As soon as Carstairs had finished speaking, he jumped onto the window ledge, and with only the least hesitation, he plunged forward into space.

I do not think I could tell you with any accuracy what Holmes or I said or did. We stared out of the window in a sort of frozen horror, and saw the little group of men gather round Carstairs's body. One of them, Wieland, I think, bent over him, though it was pretty clear that there was no hope, and then someone put a coat over him.

'Well, Holmes, we seem to have brought a liberal portion of disaster to the school,' I said.

Holmes shook his head. 'It was hardly of our making, Watson. I confess that I am surprised that Carstairs should have been implicated.'

'Yes, he seemed a thoroughly decent young chap.'

'And his background was impeccable. The Duke of Greyminster himself recommended Carstairs, on His Grace's own testimony.'

'Good Heavens! You cannot think the duke is implicated?' I asked, horrified.

Another shake of Holmes's head answered this. 'If he were, Watson, then he would hardly have consulted me in the first place. No, this poor young fellow must have started off on the right track, and somehow been tempted to evil. But how?'

'He may genuinely have believed in the objects of this secret society. World peace, and all the rest which you mentioned. After all, we do not know as yet just what the society did, do we? Donaldson, an older man, apparently a harmless old chap, may well have fooled Carstairs completely.'

Holmes seemed dissatisfied with this. 'You could be right, but I cannot quite see it. Now, what would cause a young fellow –' He stopped abruptly, and gripped my arms. 'Where is the sickroom, Watson?'

'Why? Oh, very well, I'll take you there.' I led the way down the stairs and out into the main building. As you may imagine, there was a considerable crowd of curious bystanders down there, and a good many questions were directed at us as we pushed through the crowd.

Holmes ignored questions and questioners alike, and manoeuvred me through the hall and into the comparative stillness of a corridor. 'Now, Watson.'

'This way.' I led him to the sickroom, tapped upon the door, and looked in. There was only one occupant, Miss Windlass, and I was somewhat surprised to see her slumped in a chair, and in evident distress.

Before I could offer some consolation, Holmes had brushed past me, and stood over her. 'Donaldson and Carstairs are both dead,' he said, in what I privately thought a most brutal fashion.

Miss Windlass looked up, and nodded. 'You will give me a moment?' she asked. 'I need a few personal articles.'

'Very well,' said Holmes.

Miss Windlass stood up and went into an inner room. I stared at Holmes. 'You have evidently formed your own view of all this,' I said, 'but I fear –' A loud crash from the inner chamber made me stop.

Holmes raced to the door and threw it open. He groaned aloud. 'Too late, Watson! I blame myself,' he added, as I looked over his shoulder at the inert form of Miss Windlass. 'I should have foreseen this. Though perhaps it is for the best.'

'Do not be so harsh with yourself, Holmes,' I told him. Then added, 'But I think we had best leave, before anything more happens.'

ELEVEN

'It seems pretty clear what happened,' said Holmes, as we made our way to Dr Longton's study. 'An attractive older woman, a young man away from home. The old story. And I have little doubt that some of the older boys were also encouraged by Miss Windlass. Although you will perhaps wish to let your readers think that it was all very romantic and harmless.'

'You don't know that it wasn't, Holmes!' said I. 'No need to besmirch the lady's name without knowing all the facts.'

'You may well be right,' said he.

I may add that Holmes subsequently searched the rooms of the three principals, and questioned such of the rather scared pupils as would admit to being members of the society. As he had thought, Donaldson's object had been to gain the confidence of such boys as seemed likely to rise to positions of influence – not a difficult task, given the exclusive nature of the school and the family backgrounds of the pupils – and influence them to work against Britain's interests. A mixture of persuasion and blackmail had been used, and other methods which I shall not mention here. Holmes did not reveal, even to me, the foreign power for which Donaldson and the others had worked, but the information he gleaned was passed on to those in authority, and more than one treaty was nullified and more than one ambassador was recalled shortly after. And I fancy that one or two unexplained suicides might also be put down to this investigation, though that is mere speculation on my part.

For the moment, though, we had some explaining to do to the mystified headmaster. 'That little wretch Carstairs fooled me completely,' I told Dr Longton bitterly. 'For a time I even suspected that you were at the bottom of it!'

'Not to mention Mr Tromarty, Herr Wieland, *et al*, Watson,' murmured Holmes at my elbow.

'Now, now,' said Dr Longton, laughing. 'I am not too surprised you were fooled, Doctor, for I was myself.'

'I see now, of course, that he cleverly told me only a part of the truth,' I went on.

Dr Longton nodded. 'The Whitechurch matter was entirely a concoction of Carstairs's and Donaldson's making. Carstairs came to me apparently in some distress, saying that he had brought the week's money to my study, but I was not there. He therefore left the cash on my desk, and went out of the room, subsequently leaving his own room as well. Suddenly, he told me, he recollected that the money was still there, and ran back, to find to his horror that twenty-five pounds had vanished. Well, you can imagine my own consternation. But then Donaldson came along, said he'd been to see me and I wasn't in, but he'd spotted Lord Whitechurch leaving my room, looking guilty. Of course, I never doubted for a moment what had happened, and acted accordingly.'

'Carstairs took the notes himself, put them in the boy's room,' I said. 'The object being, of course, to discredit young Lord Whitechurch, so that even if he mentioned the secret society – and that was unlikely, considering the circumstances under which he left the school, the cloud of suspicion and what have you which hung over the poor lad – had he spoken of it, still he would not be believed.'

Holmes nodded. 'Of course, they relied on you, Dr Longton, not to give their names, out of a sense of honour.'

'Honour!' groaned Dr Longton.' I have slandered an innocent boy, perhaps ruined his future completely.'

'Come, now,' said Holmes. 'It is not so bad. You have but to reinstate him to gain a reputation for fairness as well as firmness. As for the lad himself, he will dine out on the story for the rest of his days!'

'As will my two namesakes,' I added. 'But then what of poor Greville?' I asked Holmes.

'Oh, I think that is pretty obvious. He had suspected something, or someone. Probably not Carstairs, I imagine, or he would never have met him as he did. No, probably Greville had some suspicions of Mr Donaldson, let us venture, but he naturally did not wish to approach you, Dr Longton, with vague tales about a much older man. He therefore spoke to Carstairs, as being the only man of about his own age and outlook. He might, of course, have spoken to Reed, who is about the same age as well, but then Reed is married, with responsibilities, and lives out of the school. No, Carstairs was the logical choice.' He sighed. 'Poor devil! Had he spoken to Reed, or to just about anyone else, of course, all would have been well. As it was, Carstairs encouraged him, as I imagine, arranged the mysterious midnight meeting, very likely drugged the whisky – Miss Windlass keeps the key to the medicine cupboard, remember. Then I think it likely that Carstairs and Miss Windlass between them took the half-drugged Greville into the tower, assisted him to climb the stairs, for he would be heavy to carry up there, and – well, we know the rest.'

There was a moment's silence. 'Well,' I said, 'I promised to take one last lesson, and with your permission, gentlemen, I shall do so.'

'Yes,' said Dr Longton, 'your pupils await you, Dr Watson.' He hesitated. 'In some sense, sir, I shall not be sorry to see you go. But yet I have appreciated your efforts, and could wish that circumstances had been otherwise.'

I nodded, and took my leave. As I left the room, Holmes said, 'I shall see you tomorrow in Baker Street, Watson.'

I sought out my young charges. 'Well, boys,' I said, my voice catching at some obstruction in my throat as I glanced round at my pupils, 'tomorrow the new form master will be looking after you. Of course, I cannot authorize a holiday, nor even a half-holiday, but I can determine what we shall do for these last couple of hours that we spend together. I thought you might have some questions for me, and if so I shall do my best to answer them.'

I looked round the room again, to be met with silence. 'Nothing you want to know about Mr Holmes, or this sad business? Or about writing? Or just about life in general? No?'

I gazed at the sea of faces, so trusting, so innocent, boys with all their lives ahead of them, full of hopes and dreams with nothing, as yet, to sour them. I wondered what puzzles they might pose me, these young men of tomorrow, and hoped fervently that I might be able to answer them. Would they want my advice on their choice of career, my views on the relative claims of medicine, literature, and the army, or perhaps my opinions on the books then being written? I looked round again. 'Well, boys?'

Thirty-one youthful voices spoke as one. 'Tell us about the women of three continents, Doctor!'